SUBVERSION

SUBVERSION

THE ASCENSION MYTH™ BOOK 10

ELL LEIGH CLARKE

MICHAEL ANDERLE

SUBVERSION TEAM

JIT Beta Readers

John Ashmore
Kim Boyer
Paul Westman
Joshua Ahles
Micky Cocker

If we missed anyone, please let us know!

Editor

N.D. Roberts

To everyone who ever dreamed of making a dent in the universe.

— Ellie

To Family, Friends and
Those Who Love
To Read.
May We All Enjoy Grace
To Live The Life We Are
Called.

— Michael

CHAPTER ONE

<u>Base conference room, Gaitune-67</u>

The base was relatively quiet. It had been several weeks since the drama of their last mission and the team had been focused on training and getting themselves back into a routine, ready for the next mission they might be tasked with.

"I trust things are settling down there, since...you know."

General Lance Reynolds peered casually down the etheric-enhanced holo feed, into the base conference room.

Molly smirked, taking advantage of the privacy of their conversation. "What you really mean to ask is how are the Royales settling into married life?"

He grinned, shoving his cigar back into his mouth. "Busted," he conceded.

Molly pushed back into her chair at the conference table. The General used to make her socially anxious, probably on account of him being the 'boss of the universe' as she'd once noted to Oz. Somehow that had gotten back to him, and though he never reprimanded her for it, he had made her squirm when he mentioned it at the end of a meeting once. Since then, it had been as if the worst had already happened and their relationship had improved.

"He's doing fine," she told him. "I guess. I'm not quite sure how people are meant to adjust to marriage," she confessed.

Lance chuckled gruffly. "Well, it's been a while for me too, but I guess in the early days there might be power plays, arguments, tantrums. You know, the normal couple stuff."

Molly raised her eyebrows. "Yes!" she drawled, clicking her fingers in mock recognition. "Because I know *exactly* what you mean."

Lance laughed again. "Oh, boy. We reached sarcasm quickly that time, didn't we?"

"Well, if you insist on interrogating me about the social lives of my crew…"

"Quite."

"So," she continued. "I'm guessing that wasn't the only reason we were meeting?"

"No. You're correct." Lance flicked across some screens to view a file, his face taking on a more serious expression. "We have a situation."

"Oh?"

"Yes. And it's a little delicate."

Molly snorted indelicately. "When are they not?"

"This is true." He shrugged, humoring her. "But it's going to require a certain amount of discretion."

She leaned forward, intrigued. "Why?"

"Well, let's say we have intel we weren't supposed to have, about certain parties in the Federation. Then let's say that the other parties suspect we have that intel and let it ride. And then one day something happened that causes them to ask us to use that intel—that we're not supposed to have—and encouraged us to… share that knowledge with them."

Molly frowned. "Someone's trying to entrap you?"

Lance shook his head. "No. No, I don't think so. The Leath

government have more or less admitted to the situation. They just want our help sorting out one of their problems to save any further embarrassment. We'd potentially be saving them frictions with the other member states, which would be good for everyone."

Molly narrowed her eyes. "What have the Leath done now?"

Lance coughed. "You're not going to like it."

Her eyebrows flicked upwards again.

"But, the consolation is that you get to put an end to it, in a small way."

Molly braced herself.

He doesn't normally dance around mission details like this.

Sounds like it must be big.

Do you already know about it, Oz?

Nope. Nada.

"Okay," she pressed. "Out with it. What exactly are we dealing with?"

Lance sighed. "Well, it appears that a rogue faction of the Leath have been dealing in arms."

"Why is that such a surprise?"

"The arms they're dealing have come indirectly from the Leath government."

Molly opened her mouth to speak, but no sound came out. She closed her mouth and looked into the corner of the room, processing.

Lance shifted nervously in his chair.

"For what it's worth," he said, "it really does look like a rogue group, and the Leath have had problems with corruption in their government, just like any other. Believe me when I say I'm not happy about this but taking into account the greater good, it's far better that their government stays intact. They're not perfect, but there is a willingness to do better. The last thing we want to do is undermine their credibility with the Federation and their own citizens. Plus, we want them on our side."

"So what you're saying," she eventually concluded, "is that we get to take *some* of the bad guys down, but we're not to touch the governing body who started this whole exchange?"

Lance picked up his half-chewed cigar with a grimace. "Essentially."

Molly frowned. "You *are* going to deal with the government end? You know—the part where they're selling arms to terrorists?"

Lance held up a hand to appease her. "I'm already handling it. One way or another, it will be dealt with."

Molly eyed him skeptically.

"Oh, don't you worry," he finished, a stony expression settling over his handsome features, "it will become relevant at some point or another. If not politically, then in some other way. They'll learn."

"Well, ok then. What's the situation on the ground?"

"Not on the ground on this one I'm afraid. It's going to require a ship interception. We have the coordinates of when the exchange is going down. It's the only window of opportunity when we know where the weapons are going to be. We know that the Leath are buying back some arms from a Skaine group, probably to sell them at a higher rate somewhere else. It's standard practice with these groups for them to move merchandise around... sometimes in payment for other things."

Molly mulled the variables. "And you want us to grab them before the Leath get them so that the weapons don't end up back with the Leath authorities and flag that some of their weapons have been sold by their own government through back channels."

"Exactly."

She tapped her nails against the table as she put the pieces in order. "So we need to intervene before they change hands. Which means going after the Skaine ship..."

"No one said it was going to be easy."

"No. But talk about walking a tightrope. And we're going to

be doing this while the Leath are watching no doubt. That's assuming that the Skaines are the first to show up."

Lance studied her holographic image for a moment. "I've no doubt that your team can figure out how to make it work, Molly. No matter which way it turns out."

Molly sighed, racking her brains to come up with a solution. "I hope so, coz I'm coming up blank right now."

He sat up straighter, rocking in his console chair. "You'll come up with something, you always do. Well, ADAM is transmitting mission details over to Oz as we speak," he said, brightening. "Keep me posted."

Molly nodded, already partially absent as she turned the challenge Lance had given her over and over in her mind. "Yes, sir."

The image froze for a second before going blank as the holo-connection closed.

So... helping a dirty government keep its sordid little secret?

Molly heard the distaste Oz felt for the mission loud and clear. *Well, I'm not entirely jazzed about it either. But we have a job to do, and it sounds like Lance has a plan for dealing with the rest of it... at some point. I trust him.*

True. Ok. We've got the mission packet. Want me to assemble the gang?

Yeah. Sure. May as well get to it.

Lecture Theatre Three, Skóli Uppstigs Academy, Spire, Estaria

Professor Von stood in front of her second-year students. Her lesson was designed to delve into the subject without overloading the students with information. Her approach had always been to give context and motivation to the information so that it was easier to recall later.

She had experimented with telling them what was going to be examined on the end of term paper but had found over the years that this encouraged rote learning rather than the level of comprehension that these students would need for what they were being prepared for. Proper absorption and comprehension of the material took time.

In the end, she resorted to the way that took far more preparation but ultimately led to much better results. She'd spent the first ninety percent of the session establishing these details and motivations. Now she flicked the next presentation screen up, using her holo as a controller.

"Here's another study which shows the correlations we've been talking about. Bookmark this in your notes, read the analysis sections, and see if you agree with the conclusions. Make notes on where you don't agree, we will discuss this in our next session." She waited while they captured what they needed.

"Here's another."

She flicked another study with title, link and graphs onto the presentation screen.

"And another."

The students busied themselves tapping on their holo devices and capturing the links and references, so they could reference them later.

Von paced between the rows of occupied chairs. "Pay attention to the details, because your end of term project is to fantasize about how you can combine these components to make a society that functions, without resorting to existing or historic models that have failed. You will be modelling them using computer simulations and real-life starting population data."

One of the students raised his hand.

"Jeremy. Yes?"

Jeremy took a moment to formulate his question, the weight of the teacher's attention on him now. "Um... My programming isn't any good, but I think I can come up with some pretty neat ideas."

Von smiled. "It's as if I placed you to ask that question. The other part of this assignment is that you need to do it in groups of two. One person can take the programming and the other can take the abstract idea research and modelling aspects. Note that 25% of your grade will be based on how well you collaborate."

There was a muttering throughout the classroom.

Von decided there was another teaching point in there. "Anyone want to tell me why we're putting such an emphasis on collaboration?" A few hands went up. Von pointed to a brunette in the second row. "Yes, Laurel?"

The student spoke up. "Because we're preparing to exist in a society where skills can be outsourced, and collaboration is the most valuable asset when applying to a workplace."

Von bobbed her head. "Very good, Laurel. Nice to see that someone is remembering some of our first-year material."

The bell rang.

"Ok folks, start thinking about your projects now. You'll have a full briefing on it in a few weeks when the clock starts. In the meantime, please make sure you've read chapter four before next class. We'll be starting on the key components of effective governance next time."

The students pushed their chairs back and began packing up. Von disappeared behind the front bench, out of the way of the mass exodus. End of day bells were normally met with a stampede, even though these students were some of the most enthusiastic she had ever had the pleasure of teaching.

Paige sat at the back, catching up on her messages while her classmates cleared the building. She'd learned to make use of the extra minutes here and there to keep up with things.

And since trying to manage their strategy against those that wanted to see the university closed, she was having to use every spare minute she could find.

After the rush had died down, she gathered up her things and headed out to her pod to get back up to her office on Gaitune where she would continue working, waving goodbye to Professor Von as she left.

Arlene's lab, Skóli Uppstigs Academy

Bill stood over the holoscreens, hands in his lab coat pockets. The images displayed the correlations in the data he'd been working on since he joined the project.

"So you think this is significant?" he asked, watching Arlene's expression carefully.

Arlene flicked from one data set to another. "I'd say so. I think it's another piece to the puzzle." She stood back, stroking her chin. "I'm not entirely sure what it means yet, but it almost certainly means *something*."

"Maybe it's another way of narrowing down the locations of the other sites?"

"You may be right," Arlene confessed.

"Ha! Is this Professor Bailey telling me that I may have impressed her?"

She smiled, despite her efforts not to.

"This calls for a celebration!" Bill persisted. "How about dinner tonight?"

Arlene stopped.

Bill sensed the tension. "I mean, like as a thank you and everything as well…"

"I…" she hesitated.

She'd never really liked Bill. But there was no denying that him choosing to come to Estaria with them after him helping them out on the last mission was in no small part due to *him* liking *her*.

Despite her trying to let him down firmly but gently, it was almost as if it had only encouraged him further. And now it looked like dodging the question for longer wasn't going to work anymore.

There was a sharp knock at the lab door, pulling both of their attention.

"Come in!" Arlene called, hiding the relief in her voice as best she could.

The door opened, and almost eclipsing any light from the corridor was a rather large Zyhn dressed in an ill-fitting atmosuit.

"Giles told me I would probably find you up here, ol' girl." His voice was deep and commanding, yet friendly and far too familiar for Bill to be happy about this newcomer.

Bill pushed aside his lab stool, scrapping it loudly. "And who are you?" he demanded hotly.

Arlene stood with her mouth agape, unable to form the air into words.

"I'm here for Arlene," the Zyhn replied. He sidestepped Bill and held his arms out to Arlene. "It's been far too long!" he declared, embracing her.

Bill watched as Arlene let the stranger hug her. He realized that not only did these two know each other, but they were also close. He felt his face flush with embarrassment, and his chest heave with sadness as the possibility dawned on him that Arlene might be involved with someone else.

When the Zyhn finally released her Arlene seemed to wipe her face, before turning back to Bill.

"Bill, this is Ben'or. Ben'or, this is Bill... a colleague of mine."

Bill wished the ground would open and swallow him. All these weeks pining over Arlene, trying to find the right way to ask her out, and now...

Ben'or looked at him expectantly. Bill had to say something before the awkwardness became too much to bear.

"Nice to meet you Ben'or," he managed eventually. He hesitated again, trying to figure out what to say that would get him out of there. "I should probably let you two catch up."

He closed his holoscreens and headed out of the lab, the same way Ben'or had come in.

Arlene watched his retreat with a perplexed look.

Ben'or drew her attention back to him. "So, what have you been up to since we last spoke?"

She smiled. "That is a long story… one that I'd love to tell you. But I've got a meeting that I need to get to. But perhaps we could have dinner later?"

"I'd like that."

"Where are you staying?"

"I've got a hotel Giles recommended to me."

Arlene tilted her head. "He knew you were coming, then?"

"He did. It was his idea to keep it a surprise."

She narrowed her eyes. "Oh it was, was it?"

"Yes." He studied her face carefully. "Why? You don't like surprises?"

"No, no… I'm thrilled you're here. Just a little taken aback, is all. What about the council?"

"I had some leave, so I figured I'd combine it with a diplomatic visit."

She nodded in understanding. "Ah, so you're here on business?"

"A little. Just smoothing the wheels of interplanetary relations. And what good is it having friends and allies if we don't nurture that relationship?"

"You make a good case. No wonder your emperor couldn't say no to you."

"Well, from what I recall you're not bad at negotiations yourself," he chuckled. "Let me know when you're free and we'll make a plan to meet up." He hugged her again before he disappeared back out of the lab door.

Arlene watched him leave, astounded that he would suddenly show up out of the blue.

. . .

Paige's office, Safehouse, Gaitune-67

A knock on her door broke her from her concentration. Paige looked up to see Maya grinning at her. She blinked rapidly to bring her friend into focus. "Hey."

"Whatcha up to?" Maya asked. "It's gone midnight. Time to stop working and come have some fun."

Paige checked her holoscreen clock. "I guess I lost track of time."

Maya edged into the office, moving more slowly now. "What are you working on then?"

"Oh, just an idea I had in class earlier."

Maya slumped in the guest chair. "Can't believe you still find time to do class part-time and running the company. And doing a job here."

Paige shrugged, giving Maya a wry grin. "I have good people around me. They let me have it all."

Maya returned her grin. "So what's the idea?" she asked, perching down on the guest chair in front of the desk.

Paige leaned back, pushing her hair back off her face while stretching out her back. "Well, we were talking about educating the public at large about the benefits of narrowing the gap in financial wealth."

"Ha! Good luck with that!" Maya scoffed.

"Yeah, right?" Paige agreed, her face brightening somewhat as she talked. "But it got me thinking. What if we could put it in the form of entertainments, through the social channels we normally push the fashion stuff through. Make it engaging?"

Maya pursed her lips. "I think there's a danger of it becoming propaganda though. You'll lose a lot of people. Most folks like their entertainment devoid of any kind of agenda."

"Yeah, but what if it wasn't with a specific agenda. Propaganda is where you only give one argument. One side of the argument. What if we did all sides? So it's real education. Real information."

Maya thought for a moment. "You mean developing an informed populace?"

Paige chuckled. "Yeah. I know. Unrealistic. But even if we could help just one percent of folks who want to know what's going on, wouldn't it be worth it?"

Paige could see Maya's brain churning. "Yeah. But what's it going to take?"

"That's what I'm trying to figure out now," Paige told her. "We'd need to run the content as campaigns, and it would need to be well thought through."

"And then the content would need to be designed to be informative and cover all angles." Maya was getting into it now.

"Yeah. I've been drawing up some outlines and examples, and a list of folks on the ground who I could give this to run."

The conversation lulled for a moment. Paige thought about getting some air, then realized she should probably think about getting some sleep instead.

"So what about their normal work?" Maya asked. "You know, advertising the nail colors, et cetera?"

"Well, I've got a theory that if we increase the value of the content we're pushing out, we may even increase our engagement and conversion rates."

Maya arched an eyebrow at that. "Bold theory."

"Yeah." Paige wiped her face with her hands. "But we've got to do something. Things are getting rough out there. The other outlets are being bought up by the Northern Clan and pushing their agenda. There's a polarization in the messaging happening. I swear, if I were down on Estaria exposed to the crap they're pushing out through every channel, I'd be questioning which way was up."

Maya pulled her hair tie out and worked on recapturing it into a ponytail. "Yeah, it's pretty intense out there," she agreed grimly. "We've been picking up chatter on the circuit about other political manoeuvres happening behind the scenes too." She paused. "Molly is convinced that something is coming."

Paige studied her friend, her own facial expression grim now. "Yeah. I mean, why else would she agree to work with her mother?"

Maya snorted playfully. "She's a martyr for the cause! But you know, that Director Bates is something. Pieter pulled an audio of one of her 'pep talks' to her new analysts. It was not pretty."

"Oh my ancestors. I'd pay money to hear that!" Paige couldn't help but smile at what she might have said.

"No need. I'm sure he'll share it with us after a few beers. Speaking of, I think that would be an excellent plan before hitting the sack."

Maya pulled up her holo. "All right. Lemme see if we can peel him away from his MMO-RPG holo games." She started tapping a message, muttering as she typed. "I dunno what it is about those things, but it seems that Bourne and Oz have been more than a little involved in it. I can only suspect that somehow Pieter has pitted them against each other for his own amusement. I'll get him to meet us in the common area. You can do the talking once I mention it, ok?"

"You're on!" Paige brightened, getting up from her desk. The pair headed out into the corridor leaving the thoughts of the imploding domestic situation on Estaria for another day.

CHAPTER TWO

Gardner News Studios, Spire

Brad Gardner couldn't get a word in. "But Chancellor, isn't it true— Isn't it true—"

The chancellor continued to talk over the show host, loudly. Obnoxiously.

But Brad was tenacious. "Chancellor if you'd allow me to just..."

The overweight Estarian chancellor finally stopped obfuscating long enough for his chins to cease wobbling, permitting Brad to ask his question.

"Isn't it true that the decision to continue trade with Ogg is a political and economic discussion meant for the decision makers in the Senate, not military personnel?"

The chancellor sneered briefly before speaking.

"Well, this may have been true once upon a time," he sneered, looking down his nose at the interviewer, "but if we need to defend our economy then we have to do it through any means necessary. That makes it a military matter."

The host tried to match the speed of his speech. "But chancellor, that simply isn't correct. In fact, that statement is verging on treason. Military commanders aren't elected by the population to make those kinds of—"

"I can assure you," the chancellor interrupted, "that the people who love this planet the most and want to make sure that its interests are protected are the same men and women who have been serving in the armed services since before you were even born."

"Whether they love the planet isn't the question…"

Brad tried to keep the interview on track. The chancellor didn't appear to operate on logic. Instead he just reverted to the same sound-bites he'd been airing on every other show, and every other media channel, for the last week. Brad had hoped that he could get him to say something different, but it just wasn't happening.

"This is a matter of protocol and due process," Brad tried to reason. "Just because they have access to the means to put a trade embargo in place, doesn't—"

The chancellor cut over Brad again, "As I explained already, desperate times lead to desperate measures, and the Estarian economy is in dire straits. If you had missiles coming at the planets no one would question the appropriate authorities stepping in to defend you. And yet it is clear that the Ogg government is deliberately acting to jeopardize our very way of life."

"I'm sorry, Chancellor, but that statement is simply not true."

The chancellor continued talking without reference to the exhausted interviewer.

Brad exhaled, trying to keep his frustration invisible in the face of the unruly guest. It wasn't the first time that an interviewee had steamrolled him in a discussion, but professional pride stopped him from retaliating with similar tactics. He knew that made him appear weak. *Late News with Gardener* was one of the last bastions in a stand against towing the line of corporate sponsorship, but there was a limit to how much longer they were going to be able to hold out.

Already they had been criticized for having a radical approach to their discussions, and their investigators were being blocked from many of the press conferences and events in protest to their bold claims against the establishment.

The only reason the Chancellor agreed to come on the interview was for exposure. And he was getting it.

Without very much heat.

Brad pushed his shoulders back, resigned. "I'm afraid that's all we have time for tonight. Chancellor Rogen, thank you for your time."

"In other news," he continued, turning to the front, his eyes now relying on the auto-cue that had just started up again under camera one.

Out of the corner of his eye he could see the Chancellor being led off the stage, and into the blackness of the studio beyond.

Good riddance, he thought to himself, while simultaneously kicking himself for not having been able to manage the conversation better.

Base conference room, Gaitune-67

Molly strode back into the base conference room an hour later. She stopped in her tracks at the door.

Bloody hell. How did our team get so big?

Well, you've got Karina on board now. On account of her proving herself with Giles in his latest escapades. And then Arlene is up to help sort out the university fiasco. And then you've just got the usual suspects.

Molly collected herself and continued into the conference room, grabbing the only empty chair.

Joel sat across the huge table from her. She felt like he was a million miles away from her, which was pretty normal these days.

Sean and Karina sat down at the far end, to her right, clearly separate from the rest of the group. To her left Crash, Brock, Paige, Maya, Jack, and Pieter were interspersed between.

She nodded to Arlene. Arlene and Paige sat together. Molly could tell from subtleties in the body language that Paige was still enamored with Arlene's special qualities.

She's probably heard some of what has gone down on Giles's missions.

Yeah. Giles doesn't exactly keep details to himself. Especially not when he has the opportunity to show off.

Which makes me wonder why there hasn't been more gossip about-

Hahaha. You stop talking in your head, but you know I know exactly what you're thinking!

Molly felt herself blushing as she stood up. The hub of chatter died down quickly, all eyes on her now.

"Ok folks," she started, "you've probably heard that we have a new mission, hence the assembly. But we have a number of things going on right now. Not least the university issue."

She nodded in Paige's direction.

"So how about we start with that, and then we'll get down to the action hero stuff."

Sean snorted, then caught a glare from Karina. He covered his mouth and nose and then settled back down.

Paige sat up, flipping open a couple of holoscreens as Molly sat back down, giving her the floor.

"Well," Paige began slowly, "the short answer is this. We're screwed."

There was a ripple of whispers around the table.

"Despite our best efforts to beat the system, making sure we would pass every single one of their criteria, somehow we've still managed to fail. Maya is in the process of acquiring their work product, so we can see exactly what we've done wrong, but they're refusing to share it with us because it's their IP, and therefore protected by law. Allegedly. We have people on the board working the legal angle right now."

17

Molly listened intently. She noticed that she felt incredibly alone in a room full of her team.

There was quiet in the room for a few moments. Then Arlene casually raised her hand. "I may be able to help."

Molly nodded her the go ahead.

"Well," Arlene continued, "Ben'or is here, on a kind of diplomatic mission cum vacation." There were a few knowing smiles around the table.

"Go Arlene!" Brock teased. A wave of light laughter washed through the meeting.

Blushing, Arlene tried to hide her smile but to no avail. She carried on with her point. "The thing is, he's an incredibly talented diplomat."

"Bet that's not all he's talented at!" Sean interjected. He'd expected the same response as Brock got, but instead Karina elbowed him in the ribs and the laughter stopped.

Arlene ignored him. "He may be able to help. He could see things we're missing, and he may have strategies that we could use to resolve the problem. I'm sure he's dealt with worse in his position."

Molly glanced across at Joel who seemed to agree it was worth a shot. "Ok," she confirmed. "Let's read him in. I'd set a meet on Estaria with him, Gareth Jones, Paige, Maya and yourself. I'm sure if you put your heads together you can come up with something else we can try."

Arlene took a note on her holo, mostly to avoid awkward eye contact with the others around the table. Paige's face relaxed, and then she also decided to take some notes.

"Okay, next item," Molly announced.

Sean leaned forward, the playfulness gone from his demeanor. "Are you going to tell them about you pushing your will?"

She shook her head. "I don't see how it's relevant."

"They need to know," he insisted.

"Not now. Besides, we still need to test it."

Oz chipped in. **Hmm. I can set up a test.**

Molly sighed mentally. *Fine. Can I get back to running this briefing?*

Be my guest.

"Next item is a new mission from Lance."

There was shuffling from the group. Everyone sat up in sudden rapt attention.

Sean chuckled. "'Bout time we got to blowing some shit up for the Federation," he muttered. Molly glanced at him, and he simmered down again.

He's acting out?

Seems to be. Resisting domestication, I suspect.

Cute.

Molly poked at her holo and the presentation screen unfolded from the center of the table. A Leath ship appeared on it in three dimensions. "The General has asked us to intervene in a weapons trade," she explained. "It seems that a rogue Leath faction is trying to buy weapons from the Skaines. The location isn't far from here, which I suspect is why we caught the case."

Sean chuffed. "Sure. That, and the fact that the General needs plausible deniability on this—which he won't have if he sends some of his guys."

Molly narrowed her eyes at him, studying while responding. "Sure. But you do realize we're using Federation ships, Sean? Or had that escaped your notice these last few years?"

Sean shrunk back into his chair, looking sheepish. He shrugged with one hand that was resting on the table, almost abdicating his point.

Molly continued. "Our job is to show up at the exchange and meet the Skaines, so that the Leath group can't take receipt of the weapons. If they're prevented from doing the deed, I'm guessing that will reduce the charges, and allow the government to deal

ELL LEIGH CLARKE & MICHAEL ANDERLE

with the problem quietly. This has political implications, so there is zero error on this one, folks."

She paused to check that everyone was following. "We, on the other hand, will get to deal with the Skaines, who I'm told are a delightful species. They're mercenary at worst and commercially-minded at best. And the Leath are planning on either using the weapons or selling them to the highest bidder in any kind of high stakes war they can get a foothold in. The General wants the weapons taken out of circulation." She ran a hand over her hair and sighed. "But that isn't our biggest challenge. Brock, Crash, Pieter. I need you three working on the logistics of the situation. This is going to be a mid-space exchange and all we have are the coordinates of the meeting point and the time. I'd rather only have to deal with the Skaine ship so we need some way of shielding the exchange from the Leath, who will be showing up at the same time. If that wasn't enough to contend with, we need to account for one party showing up before the other."

Pieter scribbled notes frantically. Brock listened, frowning attentively. Crash's face remained expressionless, as usual.

Sean opened his mouth to speak again, this time raising his hand to shoulder level. "Does this mean we have permission to use lethal force?"

Molly rolled her eyes.

"I'm just saying," Sean continued as earnestly, as he could given his resting cynic face, "we could just blow their ship up and that would be the end of it."

Molly shook her head, but Paige interjected before she could respond. "Dude. You know that's not what we do. We bring them in, find out what we can, and then follow the situation to see if we can bag ourselves some more bad guys."

Sean screwed his face up. "I think we need to be prepared though. Just in case it comes to it."

Molly conceded. "As always. Yes. Okay, make sure we're

equipped to do that… just in case it comes to it. But it's never been, nor ever will be, our first course of action."

Sean mock-saluted. "Aye, aye, Captain!"

Molly and Paige locked eyes, a stream of communication running between them, that could be summarized in one word. "Boys!"

Molly grinned, shaking her head fondly. "Okay, any other questions?"

Karina raised her hand. "Where do you want me?" she asked, almost hesitantly.

Molly paused before she spoke. "How about coming along on *The Empress*?"

Karina's eyes lit up.

"Sounds like we'll need someone to keep Mr. Trigger-Happy in line, anyway," Molly added dryly.

Karina accepted the challenge with a nod. Sean looked a little less enthusiastic, dropping down in his seat another inch.

"Okay, we know what we need to do. Let's move out. Brock, Crash, run an ETA through Oz when you know where we stand with *The Empress*."

"Aye, Captain," Brock saluted, jumping up from his chair.

The team disbanded from the conference room in a flurry of activity, each headed out to get started on their various tasks.

Special Task Force Offices, Undisclosed location, Estaria

"All right people! Listen in!" Director Bates called over the chatter of the conference room. "Lots to get through this morning. We've had preliminary results of the analysis that some of you were involved with over the weekend, and the news isn't good." She remained standing at the head of the conference table, her presentation slides already projecting onto the room's holoscreen.

The eager students-turned-first-intake-of-special-agents in

Carol Bates' Federation-endorsed "spy school" sat in the conference room. They were suited, booted, caffeinated and ready to work.

Having graduated from Molly's Skóli Uppstigs Academy, it was hoped that they understood more of what the world needed to correct the balance that had been increasingly off-kilter in the Sark System.

Despite this, Carol somewhat doubted they understood the enormity of what they were going to face, nor the sacrifices that would be asked of them as they entered this world of intrigue. This was an aspect of their world that most of the citizens were blissfully unaware of the sacrifices of the people standing before her now would ensure they remained blissfully unaware. Their mandate was to ensure the people remained safe, with a better existence when all was said and done.

She had done her best to explain the stakes to them during her pep talk when they first joined the project. However, the more she tried to dissuade them, the more they strained at the bit to begin, relishing the challenges ahead. In the end she gave up, assuming that they would form their own opinions eventually anyway.

Just under a dozen agents waited with bated breath for their boss to read them in on everything that was transpiring in the underworld. She felt half sorry for them, these bright young things. They were initiates in a war against the corruption that permeated the shadows of the political and commercial landscape. Where the ebbs and flows which governed the trends and motivations were manipulated to massage public ego and hide the discrepancies of the avaricious. The secrets which quietly ran the existence of the civilization, impenetrable by the media, even less so to the masses who lacked the resources to pull together the pieces the agents were about to be made privy to.

The report she had studied an hour earlier showed a picture emerging in the data.

"It seems that we weren't far off with our projections," she confirmed. "Now that we have the intel to corroborate it I can tell you categorically that there is indeed a power grab happening in the heart of the Sarkian civilization as we speak. This power grab seems to be motivated and propelled by profit. Nothing new there—except that it is the single most organized movement that we have ever witnessed in the recorded history of Estaria."

She glanced at the young faces of her new agents as she spoke. With a seasoned crew she would have expected an air of tension and gravity to descend on the room. Instead she saw glints of mounting excitement in the eyes that stared back at her.

Federenials! she thought to herself. *They think that they can't fail, and that the Federation is going to step in as soon as things get too intense down here. Pah. They'll learn.*

"To that end," she continued, shaking the distracting thought of Lance Reynolds' arrogance from her mind, "the two new political appointments that were announced last Thursday are a part of this campaign. Our analysis of financial transactions over the last few months has confirmed that these were instigated, if not ordered, by the Northern Clan."

There was a muttering amongst a couple of agents off to her left. She gave them a warning glare. "Cyber taps on key suspected conspirators have also alerted us to two more possibilities. The position of the Undersecretary to the Department of Holo Media, and the Head of Cyber Communications."

One of the agents to her right raised his hand, his starched atmosuit wrinkling in an unnatural way.

"Yes, Cleavon."

"Aren't these positions already occupied?"

Carol forced herself to display a tight half-smile by way of encouragement. Molly had suggested that she try and appear more personable with the agents. "Nice catch. Yes." She held the smile as she looked back at the group. "That's exactly the case. And so, we suspect that the existing personnel will either be moved or taken care of in some other way. If there *is* a plot to assassinate them, then we've got a reason to intervene. We'll have evidence to take them down with, and may even prevent the assassinations from occurring. Anything else will be much harder to prove."

She paused and focused her attention on the three agents down the right-hand side of the table about halfway back. "Bravo team: Elroy, Dhashana, and Cleavon, you're on protecting the personnel. Charlie team: Alisha, Joshua, and Rhodez, you're on the investigation. The two teams will collaborate in order to make sure the targets stay alive, get what we need to follow the chain of command back and get the guys who are pulling the strings."

She eyeballed each of them as she spoke. "Think you're up to it?"

"Yes, ma'am," all the agents responded, almost in unison.

Carol nodded. "Good."

She poked a few of the holographic keys on her wrist holo and a presentation screen lit up in the center of the table.

"Ok, Raza and Soraya, you're on the existing appointees. One is in the Department of Near Space Communication, the head of which is Garet Beaufort. As you'll see when you look at the file, the position that has been filled is the undersecretary to the office."

Raza, the only Ogg on the team raised his hand. "Ma'am? What's our working theory on why it's the undersecretaries and deputies that are being targeted?"

"Good!" Carol applauded. "We suspect it's because such appointments draw very little media attention, but they have the same access to intel and decision-making influence. But we don't want to conclude that until we know for sure. If we can under-stand the motives behind the shuffle, then we may be able to deduce who else might be at risk."

Carol flipped her holo closed, and the presentation screen

folded away. "Raza, see if you can convince a judge to get cyber-surveillance on both of them. It would be nice to know where we stand."

Soraya, who was occupying the place next to Raza interjected. "Isn't that the Garet-guy that Molly rescued in the early days?"

Rhodez became animated. "Yeah. Before she faked her own death?"

All agents turned their full attention to Carol for the answers.

Carol pursed her lips. "I believe so," she admitted reluctantly. "Like I said, it would be nice to know whether that was a mistake or not."

Raza made a note on his holo. "I'll get right onto it, ma'am."

"Good," Carol responded. "As soon as we get permission we want to have eyes and access to both appointees. And their bosses."

Carol noticed that she had brought her mocha into the meeting and it was going cold. *Dammit.* "Elroy, I'd also like you to finish collating the data we've been analyzing over the weekend and get it onto the secure server for Molly to review."

"Yes ma'am," he confirmed.

"And Soraya, while we're waiting on the judge, could you do a download and see if there is anything new from our friends in the sky?"

Soraya nodded and made a note.

She took a quick sip of the untouched mocha. "Ok. Any other questions?" Carol asked.

The newbie agents were quiet.

"Ok, off we go. Keep me posted on any developments as they happen. Other than that, we'll reconvene for an interim briefing tomorrow at 8 am again. Dismissed."

The agents got up and scuttled back out to their consoles in their windowless office space. They were much quieter than they had been in a class at the university. This was their chance to make an impact. To shine. To catch some bad guys and maybe eventually experience all the things they admired that they heard in Molly's tales.

For this small cohort of graduates, this was a fantasy come true.

And no one wanted to do *anything* that would mess that up.

Cleavon hurried out to his desk and before he even sat down he was on a secure outside line to fix an appointment for a quiet off-book meeting with a judge who had been read in on the nature of their special task force.

He uttered the code word and waited on hold, watching around the office as his classmates hurried to execute their orders. Holoscreens jumped to life as each one settled at their enhanced and secured consoles, tapping into the network of intel and chatter that was the lifeblood of their new world.

He sat down and leaned back as the data rolled down his screen. Life didn't get much better than this.

CHAPTER THREE

"Hans, I need a word," Director Bates muttered to him quietly as his teammates left the meeting room.

Hans hung back discreetly while the others filed out before pulling out the chair nearest the door. He hadn't said a word during the meeting. Nor asked about what his assignment was. He understood he had a slightly different role to play in this organization.

Carol closed the door after the last of the agents had left. "I want you to investigate something else. It's just a hunch at this point, but some of these personnel changes are reminding me of an operative turned mercenary I used to know when I was in the field. You'll have to be extremely careful though. I want you to work closely with Philip."

As if deliberately choreographed, Philip arrived at the transparent meeting room door. He tapped on the glass before letting himself in. "Oh, you've started without me?"

"Not really," she told him. "Just getting to it."

He wandered in with a steaming cup of mocha and sat down at the table on the opposite side to Hans, leaving Carol still standing at the head of the table, as if still presenting to a group

ELL LEIGH CLARKE & MICHAEL ANDERLE

of agents. She seemed to relax a little and pulled out her own chair to sit too.

"You told him about your Sneaky Steve theory?" Philip asked with an almost flirtatious grin.

"Just getting into it," she repeated.

"Carol has been after him for years," Philip confided, hiding his grin from Carol behind his hand.

Carol eyed him amused and exasperated. "I hope you're not suggesting that my instincts are tainted by a mere vendetta?" she challenged.

Philip pantomimed being attacked for his disclosure. "I would do no such thing!"

"Good," she said firmly, reactivating the presentation holo with her wrist device. "*This* is Sneaky Steve, as we used to call him. He'll be around Philip's age now, so probably also slowing down." She dropped the comment as if it were an innocuous observation. A detail that might help her agent in assessing the threat.

"Hey!" Philip protested.

"Focus!" Carol instructed, moving swiftly on and enjoying her ability to playfully taunt him. "It took us forever to catch onto him because... well, he was so sneaky. Hence his imaginative nickname. None of his victims would be killed in the same way. And in fact, they'd often go undetected for the longest time because more than half the time we'd never recover a body."

Hans shifted slightly in his chair but kept his expression neutral as he assessed the intel on the screen.

Carol continued. "Most of those cases still officially went down as missing persons."

Hans had a hand over his face, his arm leaning on the arm of the chair. He moved his hand to speak. "How was he getting rid of the bodies so efficiently?"

"We found traces of acid at one of the victim's houses in the bathroom. We think he..."

Carol didn't finish her sentence. From the grimace on Hans' face, she didn't need to.

"Even if he wasn't involved in our disappearing government employees, if he's around then we need to do something about him. He's a nasty piece of work and needs taking off the streets."

Philip bobbed his head as Carol spoke. "Permanently," he added in.

"Which is why this is a private conversation." Carol's face grew dark. "To be clear, you are hereby authorized to use any means necessary to take this man out of play."

Hans nodded abruptly, once. "I understand."

"We'll get you access to the file while you're in the building," Philip explained, "but you won't be able to access it from anywhere else."

"Of course," Hans acknowledged.

"You'll report directly to Philip on this one too," Carol added. "Ok. That's it. Any questions?"

"No, ma'am."

"Excellent." Carol stood up. "Good luck, Hans."

Hans got to his feet too. "Thank you, ma'am." He nodded to Philip and headed out to the workstations to join his colleagues.

Carol waited for the door to close behind him. "You think he can handle it?" she asked, her gaze following him down the stairs and into the main office.

Philip took a sip of his mocha. "He'll be fine." He laughed quietly. "Reminds me of myself at that age."

Carol snorted lightly. "What? Young?"

Philip narrowed his eyes at her but thought it prudent not to continue his musings.

Ola Restaurant, Spire, Estaria

Arlene arrived at the restaurant feeling uncharacteristically flustered. The maître d' had sent her through to find her "friend."

The lighting was low, and it was a semi-casual arrangement, creating a relaxed ambiance. She recognized a silhouette over at the far window waving, guiding her in.

She wandered over between the tables, noting the ones occupied by diners. A smooth melody emanated from hidden speakers in the background and the smell of onions and garlic hung in the air.

"Ben'or!" she exclaimed, approaching his table. He stood for her, hugging her as though they'd been friends for years.

"I'm glad you made it. It did cross my mind that you might have been too tired after a full day's work and that secret off-world meeting of yours."

She waved her hand, as he pulled her chair out for her. "It wasn't secret."

Ben'or smiled knowingly.

"Ok. So, it was a little. But not for you. I have clearance to tell you something about it."

He raised one eyebrow as if he knew what was coming. Arlene was about to question his expression when their server appeared to take their drinks order.

Ben'or ordered an Estarian wine, commenting that he'd seen some documentary about it on the way over. Arlene wasn't sure if he was teasing her or if this Zhyn warrior turned diplomat really did have access to information as mundane as their farming and winery practices.

"So," he began as the waiter walked away "Do you want me to tell you about the wine we're going to drink, or would you like to invite me onto your project first?"

"How did you-?"

"Well, why else would you be given clearance to talk to me about it."

Arlene blushed. "Of course," she admitted shyly. "It's been a long day." She caught him up with the general things that had been happening before the server arrived with their wine, uncorked and poured it, and then left them to talk.

"The problem is with the university, and since you're such an excellent diplomat I just thought you'd be able to see it from an angle that maybe we haven't considered yet."

"Oh. You want me for my mind!" he teased.

Arlene frowned playfully. "What else would I want you for?"

Ben'or held up his glass to toast her. "We can begin with my mind, then." He winked at her as their wineglasses touched. Arlene felt herself flush again and tried to calm herself by taking some discreet long breaths.

It had been a long time since their Moons of Orn adventure, and though they had hit it off and promised to stay in touch, their individual duties and responsibilities had kept them from spending much time communicating. The extreme distances didn't help, and as far as Arlene knew Ben'or didn't have access to Gate technology.

All of that made her feel that it was more her responsibility to head out to see him, but then one talisman after another had dragged her on one trip after another and kept her a little too busy to be allowing herself to indulge in a romance.

But now, here they were.

Ben'or listened raptly while Arlene explained the situation with the university, and how they were about to be closed down.

"Of course, I would be honored to be of assistance," he told her when she drew to a nervous close.

"Great," she breathed. "We have a meeting set for tomorrow. We're just trying to confirm the timing since we need Paige there too, and she's the limiting factor at the moment."

"Well, as you know, I purchased a holo device for my time on Estaria, so I am contactable any time, day or night."

She grinned. "Well, we'll try and make sure you have the nights free, but there are no guarantees with Molly projects."

He chuckled. "Yes, I got that impression. Now, how about you tell me everything that I've missed since I last had the pleasure of your company."

They talked for several hours, until the restaurant was finally deserted but for a couple of exhausted staff members. Arlene stifled a yawn as they paid their bill.

"Looks like it's time to call it a night." Ben'or looked around at the empty tables set ready for the next day in surprise. "Let me get you home," he offered.

She waved her hand. "Tell you what, how about I get *you* home? You like interesting technology, don't you?"

His eyes lit up with the same enthusiasm that drew him to her when they had met the first time on his home planet. "I do indeed. Is this hush-hush technology?"

Her mouth turned up just a touch, telling him everything – and nothing at all.

Ben'or's mouth opened slightly. "Well, lead the way, m'lady," he told her with a flourishing gesture.

The pair left the restaurant, tipsy on wine and the high of each other's company.

Base workshop, Gaitune-67

Pieter and Brock clattered down the stairs to the basement. Having spent a few hours in the meeting room with Molly sifting through their options and making sure they knew the parameters of the meet, they now understood the task they had ahead of them.

It was not straightforward.

Brock, half dazed from wracking his brain, scratched at his head as he arrived in the workshop.

"So how are we going to pull this little miracle off?" Pieter asked, following him like the ever-eager assistant.

"I'm not sure yet," he confessed, waving his hand in front of one of the workshop holoconsoles. It activated his music at an ambient volume level. "I think the two biggest problems we need to solve are how to fool a Skaine ship into thinking we're their Leath contacts, and how to remain hidden from the Leath ship when that shows up too."

Pieter rubbed at his eyes. "Let's not forget we need to hide the Skaine ship from the view of the Leath ship, too. Can't have it just crashing the party."

"Dammit. That's true. And then there is the issue of what happens if the Leath ship shows up first."

Pieter thought for a moment. He slung his gear bag down on the sofa where they play video games. "If the Leath arrive first we need to be able to shield them from the Skaines in order to take their place."

"Good point," Brock agreed. "So, we need some kind of cloaking device that we can throw over a ship, and then use that for a maximum of ourselves and another ship."

Pieter frowned, trying to keep up. "Why just one?"

"Because as soon as the Skaines arrive we need to hide them from the Leath, but it doesn't matter then who sees the Leath."

"Right." Pieter narrowed one eye, as he thought it through.

"But then if we arrive first we hide the Skaines automatically, and the Leath can't see either of us," Brock continued.

Crash arrived, catching the tail-end of the conversation. "Exactly," he interjected. "Only one problem though."

"*Just* one?" Pieter asked. His hair looked extra unkempt, likely on account of him pulling at it every now and again, in a subconscious attempt to keep the variables straight in his mind.

"If we're under a cloak, then our instruments won't be able to see anything that's outside the cloak," Crash explained grimly. "Our tech is good, but not that good."

Brock slapped a hand to his head. "Shit. He's got a point."

Pieter shrugged. "So, I guess we're back to plan B then."

Brock and Crash looked at him quizzically.

Pieter grinned. "Magic wand."

ELL LEIGH CLARKE & MICHAEL ANDERLE

Crash didn't react. Brock chuckled in amusement. "If only those were Federation-issue. I think we're just going to have to do it blind. Unless we can come up with another way. Either that, or we come up with a brand-new technology before we get our marching orders."

"No small feat," Pieter mumbled.

The three debated the technical details of the issue for a few more minutes before making a decision.

"I think," Brock decided, "that our best course of action right now is to focus on getting the cloaking device working. Pieter, you wanna help me?"

Crash looked hurt for a moment. Brock noticed immediately. "I need you to make sure we can get the ship's forcefield up and looking adequately Leath-like."

Crash took a deep breath, his face relaxing somewhat. "I'm not sure I even know what a Leath ship looks like these days. I know we had to memorize it for Fed training when we started flying these babies, but it's been a while."

Pieter checked something on his holo. "I think they'll have the program already on the server somewhere. So, it's just an upload. Emma will be able to help check that it's current and not going to blow our cover."

Crash headed off in the direction of the daemon door. "Guess that means that our MMO-RPG tournament is off the table for tonight.

"'Fraid so," Brock confirmed. "Someone should let Bourne know though," he added, a little awkwardly.

"Bagsy not me," Crash muttered without hesitation.

Pieter and Brock stood looking at each other. Brock reacted first. "I've got to check the auxiliary power on *The Empress* before we run the program, which means you have time before I need you."

"But…" Pieter protested, watching Brock move to collect up

the tools he was going to need. "He can be such an asshole when he doesn't get his own way!"

Brock shrugged. "You can treat it as an opportunity to teach him some emotional intelligence," he suggested in his most helpful tone.

"But…"

Brock turned and slapped the top of Pieter's arm confidently. "You've got this."

Pieter shriveled. "Dude…"

Brock closed his toolbox and hauled it onto his shoulder. "You can do it. Get resourceful." He headed off in the direction of the daemon door too.

Pieter slumped down on the stool and opened the console to communicate with Bourne, who may or may not have already heard them talking about him. He hesitated, wondering if he could ask Paige to intervene and make their excuses for them.

That was when he had another idea.

He typed a message onto Bourne's server, the place where they'd agreed they would call him from if they wanted to find him.

Bourne responded through the workshop audio almost immediately. "'Sup, Pieter? You ready to play?"

"Good news and bad news, Bourne."

"Oh? Give me the good first."

Pieter mentally crossed his fingers. Bourne was always angling to help on their cases. Hopefully this tack would get him off the hook. "I may have an opportunity for you to help with some mission stuff, if you're game."

"What was the bad news?"

"Everyone else is super busy trying to get things ready for an urgent op."

There was a long pause. Pieter wondered if Bourne was doing it deliberately as a manipulation. He had been watching an incredible amount of drama from the archives.

"Oh," he said eventually.

Pieter felt himself holding his breath. "So, are you in?"

"Yeah. What do you need? My hacking is nearly as good as Oz's now. I managed to read fragments of his personal logs the other day."

Pieter paused thinking what that meant. "You mean, you read his diary?"

"I did."

"Bourne! You know that's personal."

"That's what makes it interesting!"

Pieter's head fell into his hand. "Okay, I'm intrigued to know what an AI would be writing about, but right now we have work to do. Do you think you could help me find out everything we might need to know about the Leath and the Skaines? We're going to be engaging them on an op and none of us have really had much contact with any of them."

"No problemo," Bourne told him, his synthetic voice more animated now. "I'll just need to piggyback off Oz's connection to the Federation servers. Or... I *could* go the route of hacking the Estarian and Ogg government files on their interactions."

Pieter's head remained in his hands. "Fuck my life," he mumbled.

"What was that?"

"Nothing. I was just realizing that all of a sudden I have more empathy for Molly's predicaments when it came to establishing morality for herself and Oz in the early days."

"I don't see how that is remotely connected to what we were just talking about. You know there are a host of human ailments that result in the deterioration of the trail of thought. Have you experienced any other symptoms? You might need to be checked out by a medical professional."

Pieter took a deep breath. This was going to be a long night...

CHAPTER FOUR

Kitchen, Safehouse, Gaitune-67

Molly padded into the kitchen, half-awake. It had been a long night of preparation for the mission and she only switched off her holo after Oz insisted that everything else that needed to be done could only be hindered by her interference.

She eyed the mocha machine as she ambled past it. It used to be her friend. Well, if she were totally honest it was more like one of those love-hate relationships, since when she was hooked she couldn't contemplate functioning without its sweet nectar. However, being somewhat old and decrepit it never did make morning mocha without a fight.

Now she was free of the abusive relationship she was able to resist its torment and head straight for the filtered water which she would boil and add various teas to depending on her mood.

Today was a lemon day, she decided, plopping a wedge into a cup and flicking the kettle on.

"Looks who's up without a wakeup call!" Joel strode into the kitchen.

Molly glared at him. "Have I ever mentioned I hate morning people?"

He chuckled firing up the various kitchen devices that would allow him to make whatever his morning concoction was going to be that day. Sometimes he made smoothies, other times soups. Sometimes, he even cooked protein substitutes. Molly didn't keep track. It was all too much to contemplate before she'd done some work and got the day underway.

"Can I interest you in a green mocha smoothie?" he asked.

She shook her head. "No thanks. I wanna get dressed and then see what the situation is downstairs."

Joel was already biting into a piece of fruit. "Ah, yes. It was late when I heard Brock and Crash come up to the safe house. Just seen Pieter too. He looked like a zombie."

Molly frowned. "Going to bed or getting up?"

"He was in pajamas, so he was getting up I believe."

"Ok good. I'd told them not to stay up all night." She poured her water on her lemon and started to head out.

"Hey," Joel called after her. "I know there is a lot going on, what with the university and your parents and everything, but if you wanna talk?"

Molly shrugged. "Nothing to say… unless you've got a way to fix it all?"

Joel sighed. "I haven't. But… you know. I'm here."

Molly turned back and plonked her mug on the table. She headed straight for Joel and threw her arms around his middle in a bear hug.

Completely taken aback, he nearly lost his balance. He held her for a second. He couldn't see her face, and he didn't know what was going on. All he knew was that she was allowing him a moment—and that was huge.

For both of them.

Sorry to interrupt Molly, but…

Molly peeled herself away from Joel's torso. Joel braced himself for her shutting him out. He glanced down at her and saw that her eyes were distant, but not teary. And then he realized. "Oz?"

She nodded. "What is it, Oz?"

His voice came over the kitchen intercom. "All systems are prepped and ready for take-off whenever you non-data entities are ready to get your asses moving."

Joel sniggered. Molly couldn't help but smile. "Thanks, Oz. We'll get our slow, carbon-based suits moving and ready to go. Put the word out to the team, would you?"

"All over it," he confirmed.

Molly shook her head and released Joel, who just seemed happy for the contact. She headed back out of the kitchen, picking up her mug on the way. "This life-form isn't going to dress itself!" she joked as she left.

Joel chuckled away to himself and continued making his breakfast. No way was he leaving on an empty stomach. The machines could wait...

Aboard *The Penitent Granddaughter*, Agresh Quadrant

Nickie eyed the anxious-looking Skaine carefully.

"All right Durq, are you sure you're up to this?"

"Yes. Yes. Of course. This is, after all, what you rescued me for." He shifted his weight from one large foot to the other.

Nickie plonked herself down in the pilot seat and threw her feet up on the now-redundant console. "I think we need to clear that up, actually," she told him. "Grab a seat." She pointed at another console chair in the cockpit.

Durq shuffled toward it and delicately sat down.

"You seem to think that the only reason I rescued you was because you could be useful."

Durq nodded respectfully. Politely, even.

No doubt he's as whipped as Skaine come, Meredith.

Well, it sounds like he's been through an awful lot. Even his rescue situation would have been enough to traumatize a normal human. Thankfully Skaine neurology is a little more robust.

You're such a pussy for an EI that isn't even meant to have emotions.

I have empathy algorithms. It makes my interface-

Whatever. Lemme sort out one pussy at a time...

"Well, that's not quite true," Nickie explained slowly. "The reason I rescued you was because you were an innocent in all that kerfuffle. And I wanted those bigoted bullies to pay. And pay dearly. For what they did to you, and the others. Do you understand?"

He nodded. "I think so. So, you did it for justice?"

"Yeah. Albeit my own twisted sense of justice. But I guess since I'm the captain that's the only type of justice we need to worry about."

You're sounding more and more like your aunt each day.

All right, Meredith. When I need an intervention on morality—or anything else—I'll ask for it. Stay on task.

Oh, I am on task. If you look at the screen you'll see that I'm already tracking an incoming ship. Looks Federation though, under the shields filter. Federation tech.

Shit. You're kidding. Out here in the boondocks?

Affirmative. Although, they're emitting the correct signal for it to be the Leath we were expecting.

Are you sure?

As sure as the signal can be.

So, what are we meant to conclude?

Nothing yet. Let's see what happens.

"Ok, Durq-the-Skaine," Nickie continued, "you're going to be up sooner than we thought you would be."

The new crew member shifted nervously on his seat, but Nickie was already on her feet, flicking through console screens.

"Ok, here's what we're going to do. Just like we rehearsed.

You're going to stay on camera, and Meredith is going to keep flicking the screen as if we have a faulty transmission. That'll stop them getting a really good look at you. So I can do the talking, through the voice distortion filter, and you can look like the one talking."

Durq's already wrinkled and bumpy face contorted even more. "I'm up for this... but... are you sure this is going to work?"

Nickie rolled her eyes. "Of all the Skaines I could have been landed with, I get the scaredy-cat."

Play nice. He's doing us a huge favor.

And getting a cushy number in return.

"Where's Grim?" she called out loud.

"Here!" Grim appeared at the door to the cockpit, out of breath, with crumbs around his mouth.

"Found time for a snack, did we?"

"Well, I was starving. All of this prep for intrigue was making me hungry. Plus, I thought I'd whip up some pie for later. You know, when we're done."

Nickie's voice softened. "Well... Yes, that sounds like it could be a good idea. For later. With a nice pint of that beer."

Her eyes defocused for a moment, probably thinking about the food and beer. A second later she seemed to snap back to reality.

"Ok people, we're up! Meredith is tracking the exchange ship in. We need to stay out of sight. So, if you're going to be in here, you need to come to this end of the cockpit, out of sight of the camera. So get your Yollin ass over here or get out."

Grim dusted his mouth off and hot-footed it over to the corner where Nickie was standing. He perched across the nearest console chair.

Nickie checked the screen that would provide the video screen, and then pulled him another three inches out of view.

"Sorry," he muttered.

Meredith's voice came on over the intercom this time, instead of just inside Nickie's nanocyte-enhanced head. "Okay. They'll be here in about a minute. They're already opening comm channels. Are you sure you don't need to talk this through again?"

"Meredith!" Nickie growled out loud. "I know I've been AWOL for a while, but I know how to do a fucking exchange. We just need to get them on board at the cargo hold, where Durq will meet them. Then we'll go from there. It's not fucking rocket science."

"Go from there? Huh. You know your grandfather would have had three or four different scenarios mapped out. And then he'd have his team fully briefed on each one."

"Well, I'm not my grandfather. I'm my own person."

"Masquerading as your aunt no less."

"Meredith, this really isn't the time to be critiquing my life choices. *Or* my operational methodologies."

"Right. Well, you just let me know when it is an appropriate time."

"I will. Heads up, it'll be sometime between now and, hmm... lemme see... around the same time Hell freezes over!"

"You have incoming," Meredith reported coolly.

Nickie pulled again at Grim's neck, making sure he was out of the frame. "You're up Durq."

Durq stood in the center of the cockpit now, looking as weedy and nervous as the day she had rescued him from a hellish inferno. He twiddled his fingers just below the frame. Nickie shook her head in frustration and picked up the microphone.

"This is the vessel *Your Future's Devine*... You're talking with Commander Durq. Identify!" she ordered in her deepest, gruffest Skaine dialect.

I hope your voice alteration is doing some work on this. Any lower and I think I'll break my vocal chords.

It will convince them, easily. I assure you.

. . .

Hangar Deck, Gaitune-67

Molly stood on the hangar deck, waiting for Paige and Maya to arrive. She saw them emerging not from the safe house, but from the direction of the base's conference rooms and labs. Presumably they had been in Paige's office, working.

"You all set?" Paige asked as she approached.

Molly watched Pieter carrying his gear on board *The Empress*. "I think that's the last of us," she confirmed, nodding in his direction. "You all set for your meeting later?"

Paige pulled up her holo. "We absolutely are. We've been brainstorming possible angles. It's going to be good to get another set of eyes on it for sure."

"Good. And the legal position?" She glanced over at Maya who had been following that up.

"Moving at the pace of lawyers still," she explained. "I can't even get an initial read. But there is a guy that we've managed to get a call with. I've heard from a few sources he's a brilliant legal mind. If there is a way out of this, he'll find it."

Molly pursed her lips. Her complexion was pale as if she was tired and run down. The stress around the university situation probably wasn't helping, Paige realized.

"Don't worry, Mollz," Paige told her, placing a hand on her arm. "Let us worry about it. You need to stay focused," she reminded her, looking back up at *The Empress*.

Molly smiled. "You're right. I appreciate everything you're doing. And thank the others for me when you meet, yeah?"

"I will," Paige promised. "Just get out there and get the bad guys."

Molly hugged each of them quickly and then headed down the side of the ship to the invisible steps. Paige and Maya waved and then hurried back in the direction of the office. There was much to prepare. Bringing Ben'or on board, Paige wanted to make sure that they had all their ducks in a row in order to make a good impression.

. . .

Room 434, Skóli Uppstigs Academy, Spire, Estaria

Later that afternoon, the group sat around the table in a smaller classroom in the main building. Disposable mocha cups littered the table, along with screwed up napkins and holoscreens that had been left open as they tried to figure out the solution.

Gareth Jones explained his latest thinking on the issue. "I think the root cause is that we're just making too many waves. We've had a few graduates go out into the workplace and already they're rising to positions of responsibility. They're questioning everything, changing established practices to better serve the people. It's making a difference and the powers that be are feeling threatened. Ultimately, we're victims of our success."

Paige nodded sadly, untidy wisps of her hair falling around her face. "Never saw that coming."

Ben'or fitted a lid back onto his empty cup. "So who are they, and what do they want?" His tone was that of a guru. Despite the simplicity of the question, just because it came from Ben'or it seemed that it had more wisdom to it.

Gareth sighed, leaning back in his seat. "It's difficult to say really. The order for the H&S investigation most certainly came from the Senate. That means we're looking at people in the planet's leadership who have a lot to lose if we undo the current preferential system."

"Well then, our solution needs to target them. Make it worth their while to leave us be," Ben'or explained simply.

Gareth shrugged. "There's no way we can do that. We don't know who is instigating it, or why. *Or* what they hope to gain specifically. We're assuming we're dealing with an ideology. That's very difficult to counter."

Ben'or nodded his huge head sagely. "It is. But they think they're going to gain something from what they're doing. If we are able to give them that in a different way, then we may well be able to diffuse the situation and repeal the order. We just need to figure out the who, and then find out what is more important to them."

Arlene tapped her finger on the table. "You know," she mused thoughtfully, "this is a case for more information. If we had more intel, we'd have somewhere to go."

Ben'or nodded. "Exactly," he said, tapping the table gently too, subconsciously mirroring her.

She pursed her lips for a moment before speaking again. "I think this might be a good exercise for our graduate analysts."

Gareth looked at her with an expression like he was trying to do long division in his head.

"Analysts?" Ben'or queried.

Arlene nodded. "Well, you know what we do here?"

"Yes."

"Well, some of our graduates went out into the world. But some were recently sent to a 'sister' organization. We affection-ately call it Spy School because it is headed up by the head of clandestine services—"

"Who also happens to be Molly's Mom," Paige interjected with a grin.

Ben'or's eyebrows jumped. "You're serious?"

Arlene nodded. "I'm afraid so. But the good news is that these kids have access to Federation technology, processing power, and have been trained to make the smart call. They're already proving to be quite an asset to what we're trying to do… and given what you've suggested, it sounds like they could also be the key to helping us narrow the problem down."

She made a note. "If we're all in agreement I'll reach out to Carol tonight and see what we can get rolling."

Everyone nodded.

"Great. Anything else?" she asked.

"I don't think so," Gareth concluded. "Let us know what she says, and perhaps we can reconvene in a few days?"

"Sounds good," Arlene confirmed.

Within a few minutes the meeting had been closed and Paige and Maya were heading down the deserted corridors together back to their pod.

"Well, at least there is hope," Maya mumbled, attempting optimism through her fatigue and worry.

"Yeah."

"You ok?"

"Yeah fine. Why?"

"You seem distracted."

"Oh… I was just thinking. I think I'm going to try and get a few hours of work done before I crash tonight."

"It's already getting late."

"Yeah, but I've got some ideas I wanna try out in the business. Last ditch attempt to counter the downward pull of futility." Paige moved her head as if mocking her own melodrama.

Maya giggled. "Wow! Existential for this time of the day!"

"I know," Paige confessed, more lightly now. "I've just been thinking. Von's classes always get me thinking."

"Ah, the raison d'être of education!"

"Exactly!" Paige concurred. They clattered down the steps of the side exit from the building and hopped into the waiting Pod.

"As long as you don't work too hard," Maya warned as they buckled in. "I'm going to finish up some messages and then chill. Brock said something about group gaming later. Apparently with Oz's new capacity he can run some pretty incredible immersion graphics that are mind-blowingly disorientating."

Paige rolled her eyes. "Sounds like fun though," she admitted.

Maya grinned. "Yeah, especially when Bourne gets involved and changes the game dynamics on the fly—and then Oz and Bourne end up arguing. They're so funny!"

The tension from the meeting left them as they ascended into the twilight, returning their minds to their home and friends.

CHAPTER FIVE

Aboard _The Empress_, Agresh Quadrant

The cockpit held the hum of quiet research. Pieter sat at the console closest to the back wall, holo screens out and diligently researching everything he might need to know about the Skaines, their ships, and their systems.

He cocked his head, then straightened up and turned to Brock. "Dude, how are we planning to get on board once we find it?"

Brock swiveled round in the navigator's console chair. "Huh?"

"The Skaines have compatible shuttles which dock into their ships, so they can move from one ship to another, or from ground to space. We haven't got one of those shuttles."

Brock's face contorted. "Shit. I hadn't thought of that. All the work we were doing on the forcefield and the cloaking device…" He grinned and pointed at Pieter. "Good catch though!"

He turned back to Crash, who remained stoic and motionless but for the flicking of his eyes over the console panel and the odd movement of his fingers on the controls. "You reckon this should be an ops team issue."

Crash smirked.

Brock scratched his head and turned back to Pieter. "I don't think that would fly with them." He paused, realizing his pun. "Get it?"

Pieter sniggered. "Yeah. Funny. Ok, lemme go talk to them."

He slipped down from his console chair, flicking the open holoscreens closed. Deep in thought, he headed out to the lounge to find Joel and Jack sitting toward the far end.

He explained the problem. Joel rubbed at the stubble on his chin. "Hmm. I'd not thought that bit through," he confessed. "Although… I don't suppose there is any problem with using the pods."

Pieter chuckled and slapped his palm against his head. "Sometimes I think I overcomplicate things!"

Jack grinned at him. "Sometimes we need someone who can deal with the complex."

Pieter blushed and scuffed at the floor with his plimsole. "Thanks," he said quietly.

Jack flashed her confident smile at him. "You need to start taking more credit for what you bring to this team," she told him.

Joel nodded. "Yeah. You're doing good stuff. And we should have thought of it too. We were kinda distracted with the strategy of how to communicate with them and the various ways that could play out."

Pieter cocked his head, curiously. "What are the plays?"

Joel grunted. "We have a number of them depending on whether they respond to us as Leath or whether they discover that our shields are only projecting the illusion of a Leath ship."

Pieter's eyes widened. "What if they're onto us?"

Joel shrugged. "I think that was play number 2b."

Jack nodded in confirmation.

He continued. "We start by hailing them in Skaine. Then, if they respond we get into a dialog, and tell them we suspect them of being here for an illegal weapons trade and that we're here to take them in."

Pieter's brow furrowed skeptically. "When have we ever taken anyone in?"

Joel jutted his bottom lip out. "First time for everything!"

Pieter glanced up and down the length of the lounge. "Where would we even put them? We haven't got holding cells, and my research has shown that these guys are huge! And powerful. No way you can restrain them with the usual arm restraints. Not without them killing you first."

Sean popped up over the chair in front of them. "That's because we're never going to be able to restrain them. I think we all know this. These guys aren't going to be taken alive."

Joel tried to suppress a sigh. "We need to at least try and do it by the book."

Sean grinned. "Which is why you've got the right equipment to do it? Oh no... I don't see us dragging a holding cell large enough to hold a full Skaine crew!"

Joel pressed his lips together and gave Pieter a pained look. "He has a point," he conceded.

Pieter still looked perplexed. "So how is this really going to go down?"

"Well," Joel explained, "going by the probabilities Oz ran up for us, the most likely scenario is that we end up fighting for our lives."

"I see," Pieter muttered.

Joel had expected him to be a little more anxious. Perhaps it was his preoccupation with the practicalities, or perhaps this once-green kid was starting to acclimatize to operational reality.

"So that's why Crash and Brock were spending so much time reinforcing the force field. And hooking up back up power cells?" he mused.

Joel bobbed his head. "Yep. You got it."

Pieter shrugged. "Ok. Well, that's good to know." He started back toward the cockpit. "I'm actually quite curious to meet a Skaine." And with that, he wandered off.

Jack exhaled sharply as if she'd been holding it.

Joel looked at her. "You think he's ok?"

"I think he's embracing his role." She shrugged. "I mean, he's never going to be a meat-head like Mr. Royale…"

Sean glared at her.

"But," she continued, "he's actually showing signs of being a damn good operative. A bit more time to grow into his paws, and maybe a few hundred hours in the gym, and he'll be pretty formidable in the field."

Joel smirked. "Aww. Our little boy is growing up…"

Sean rolled his eyes and slumped back down into the seat behind.

Karina detected a hint of frustration. "Everything ok?"

"Yeah," Sean gruffed. "Just need to watch my back. Sounds like boy wonder over there is after our jobs."

Karina chuckled. "Well, would it be so bad if you got to take a back seat now and again?"

Sean looked at her sideways. "This is where it begins. The beginning of the end of a beautiful career."

Karina chuckled, slapping him playfully on the arm. "No silly. We talked about this. I'm happy running around the galaxy running missions. Especially now I have you."

Joel appeared over the top of the seat in front of them. "Don't suppose you have a sick bag? I think I'm gonna hurl!"

Laughter erupted in the lounge as Sean took a playful swipe at Joel. Even Molly chuckled from the other side of the ship where she was working.

Hey?" Sean poked his head back up. "Anyone going to tell Pieter that it's Leath that are the vicious big ones, not Skaines?"

Director Bates's office, Special Task Force Offices, Undisclosed location, Spire

The holo connection opened.

"Carol," Arlene stated by way of a greeting.

"Arlene," Carol responded. There was a serious lack of warmth and genuineness in her voice. Arlene felt it with every fiber of her being. But she didn't have to like the woman for her to help save the university. After all, it was Carol's daughter's project, so it wasn't as if Carol was exactly doing *her* a favor.

"Long time."

"It has been, yes. How are things?" Arlene asked, genuinely curious what this woman had been up to recently to be brought in on a Reynolds-sanctioned project.

"Very good, thank you," she responded. "Interesting to be working on the same side of the Federation."

Arlene tried to smile. "Well, we all knew this day would come."

"Oh, we did, did we?"

Arlene's fake smile faded, despite her best efforts. This woman was just as curt and destructive as she had always been. And giving her their version of Spy School obviously wasn't helping her ego. "Well, anyway," Arlene said, getting down to business, "I'm reaching out because it looks like our attempts to keep the university safe have proven unsuccessful. They've failed us on the grounds of health and safety, so they'll be issuing a closure notice any day now. We have the vacation break to turn it around."

"I see. And how can Clandestine Services be of assistance?"

"Well, I was thinking your new team of analysts might be able to help. We're trying a new approach, finding out exactly who is behind it—"

"And shooting them?"

"Er. No."

Arlene closed her eyes for a moment willing herself not to consider the idea after all she heard being taught on the curriculum.

"No," she repeated firmly, as if trying to convince Carol rather than herself. "No, what we need to do is find out who and then figure out why, and then find another way-

"To leverage them?" Carol offered.

Arlene considered the words for a moment and then nodded. "Sure," she said. "And then leverage them."

"Ok. Sounds pretty standard to me. Any idea who we're dealing with? Any leads? Names?"

Arlene shook her head. "Only that it comes from within the H&S department in local government. We're already pursuing legal angles, so we can send over the details involved in case there is a lead amongst the rubble."

"Yes, that would be useful. I'll give you the address for a secure server we can both access."

"Ok."

"Anything else I should know?"

"At this point? I don't think so. We'd just really appreciate any light you can throw on it."

"Ok. Leave it with me. No promises, but we'll see what we can do."

"Thanks, Carol."

"Sure thing, Arlene. Good to see you." Her tone had all the sincerity of an Uptarlung car salesman.

"You too," Arlene responded as generously as she could manage.

Arlene shook the thoughts from her head and closed the remaining holoscreens at her desk. She got up from her darkened home office and ambled through to the living room, following the light, and faint sounds of movement. Ben'or sat on the sofa waiting for her. He'd opened a bottle of whiskey. He got up and handed her a glass.

"Long time since I had a good Yollin whiskey," he told her. "One of the many things I missed since we parted ways."

Arlene took the glass, and smiled, lightly touching the rim of her glass to Ben'or's. "One of the many things," she repeated.

. . .

Aboard *The Empress*, Agresh Quadrant

Crash's voice sounded over the intercom in the lounge. "Okay, we're up in thirty seconds. Molly, your presence is requested on the bridge."

Molly stood up from her seat. "No rest for the wicked," she muttered dryly to Joel, who was sitting on the other side of the aisle. He took that as his cue to accompany her and the pair headed up to the front of the ship.

They stepped into the room to find Crash and Pieter looking serious and deep in focus. Brock sat at the back on one of the spare console chairs. "They're hailing us. Thought you had better take over at this point."

Molly nodded. "Ok Oz, you're up?"

Molly sat down next to Crash in the Navigator's chair. Crash handed her the microphone. She took a deep breath.

"Greetings? *Your Future's Divine*, do you read?"

The guttural sound of Skaine came back over the audio. "They're sending a video feed."

"Shit. We're not set up for that. Keep it to audio only at this end, but put them on screen."

The screen ahead of them flashed up with a grainy, intermittent image of a lone Skaine standing in the middle of the ship's bridge.

"This is the vessel *Your Future's Divine*. You're speaking with Commander Durq. Identify!" the Skaine demanded.

Motherfuckers... They don't mess around. I thought we were meant to be on the same side.

It's the Skaines' way. Even in an exchange like this, they see it as a battle. And even a negotiation is a situation where you have an opponent rather than a collaborator.

"This is the Leath contingent," she spoke out loud. Oz worked to translate it into a native Leath tongue as he fed it through the intercom.

Too weak. You need to be more aggressive, else they're

going to catch on.

Fuck. I dunno how to do aggressive. Get Sean up here.

On it.

"I have no interest in your difficulties. Are you here to do a deal or what?"

The coarse Skaine language rang through the cockpit, only to be translated on-screen a few seconds later by Emma.

Molly's eyes scanned the translation. "We are," she announced more confidently. "But I'd like to see some proof of what you're carrying."

"By all means." The flickering video feed jumped again. "Perhaps you'd like to send an away team over to our cargo holding."

Molly removed her finger from the transmit trigger on the microphone and glanced at Joel. "It's too risky."

Joel shrugged. "I don't see what choice we have. We need to get eyes on those weapons."

Molly was thinking fast. "They're going to see that we're not Leath."

"You can pre-empt that."

"Shit. I'm going to regret doing this." She lifted the microphone up to her lips again and hit the transmit button. "I'll send a handful of human slaves. You'll appreciate that they are expendable."

The Skaine reacted on the video. A moment later the audio caught up. "You can send two. Any more and we'll kill the excess. These are our terms."

Joel rolled his lips and nodded in grim agreement to what she was doing. Sean came bounding up the steps and into the cockpit.

"What did I miss?" he hissed to Joel.

Joel whispered in his ear. "Just that Molly needs to be more forthright with her communication manner with Skaines. And that she's about to send an away team of human slaves to check out the merchandise."

Sean's eyes filled with concern. "On the ship that we're ready to go to blows with?"

"Yep," Joel admitted. "Dunno how else to avoid it… short of opening fire here and now."

Sean shook his head. "Fuck. I'm gonna regret this."

Joel clamped a hand on Sean's shoulder. "Don't worry. I'll come with you."

Molly raised a finger to the pair. "I'm coming too."

Sean shook his head. "Absolutely not. You need to stay put. You and Oz need to keep this facade going from here. You can't do it from down there. Plus, if anything happens, someone needs to give the order to fire on the ship."

"Not if you're still on there."

Sean looked at her sternly and maneuvered her into the nearest console chair. "Molly, we've been through this. And *you've* been through the Federation modules on this type of encounter."

"You've been reading my files?"

He leaned on the armrests of the chair, commanding her full attention. "Who do you think Lance shares them with?" he grinned.

Molly scowled. "I don't like any of this. Including your back-door relationship with my boss," she added pointedly.

Sean straightened up. "Well, get used to it. And take it up with the boss when we get back. In the meantime, you know what needs to happen."

Molly sighed. "So what? You and Joel?"

Sean nodded. "Yeah. Karina and Jack can stay here in case we need to do something more sophisticated. Best we're not all committed to the situation."

Molly slumped in the chair, deflated. "You're right. It's the smartest move."

Karina appeared at the door. "Well, I think the smartest move would be letting me go down with Sean. We make a great team, and that means you can keep Joel here to run any other ops that come out of the mix."

Molly noticed the protest in Sean's eyes. But she also noted that Karina had a point. "Ok," she agreed. "Sean and Karina head down and check out the weapons."

She shrugged at Sean. "It's the smartest move," she added, grinning.

Aboard *The Penitent Granddaughter*, Agresh Quadrant

"They're sending humans," Nickie repeated, tapping a finger impatiently on the console she was still perched on.

"Hang on," Grim interrupted. "I thought we were expecting Leath? What are the Leath doing working with humans?"

Nickie shrugged. "They're saying these are human slaves. Which, honestly, would be more appropriate for a Skaine crew to enslave. But if these Leath are in with the bad boys then I wouldn't put anything past them. They may have picked up some bad habits."

Grim clambered down from the console chair he had been resting on. "So, you're not suspicious?"

"I'm always suspicious," Nickie shot back. "But Meredith has confirmed they're broadcasting the correct code. It could be legit. Well, as legit as an illegal arms trade can be, I guess."

She thought for a moment, kicking her boot against the under-panel of the console. "I think we just need to see it through. Besides, what are they going to do? Take command of the whole ship? With just two humans? Against me? And the reinforced battleship cargo hold doors?"

Grim flinched at the thought of the ship coming under attack again. "Right. So you're *not* worried?" he clarified.

Nickie slipped down off the pilot's console and strode across the room. "Skeptical," she admitted. "But not worried. Let's make sure the bots have moved the gear into the right cargo bay so we're ready."

She slapped a nervous looking Durq on the arm. "Act natural, man. We don't wanna spook them."

Nickie disappeared out of the door, followed by Grim trotting after her. Durq took a deep breath and followed, trying to keep up with everything that was going on. This wasn't the life he was used to, and Nickie played things far too fast and loose for his liking.

Cargo bay, Aboard *The Penitent Granddaughter*, Agresh Quadrant

"Okay," Nickie grunted, shifting the last of the crates into place. "That should do it."

She straightened up and exhaled. "We don't want to tip our hand, Durq." She turned to talk to him, and he wasn't there. She spun round to see he was hanging back again by the door. "Get over here!" she yelled to him.

Durq scuttled over, his hunched over Skaine-mass moving in a way that his physiology just wasn't designed for. Skaines were meant for aiming guns and shooting, for wreaking mayhem while laughing at their foes and calling them names. Not scuttling and easily skulking behind tiny door frames.

Nickie slammed her fists onto her hips. "Come on now. It's really quite simple. You don't want to be letting them know that these are the only weapons we have. These are samples."

The Skaine nodded.

"Say it with me," she instructed.

"*Sam-ples*," she mouthed.

He copied, saying it slowly.

"Ok. And we're going to run this con as if these other crates are all filled with the same merchandise. Ok?"

Durq nodded. "Got it." He paused. "What if they want to

check them though?" he asked, pointing at the arrangement of crates she'd been shifting around the cargo hold.

"You redirect," she responded. Her face changed to mimic an indignant Skaine. *"How dare slaves question the Skaines! Or… Do the cattle want to be ripped limb from limb for their insolence?"* Her face relaxed a little. "Just hurry them along to make the deal. Whatever it takes." She slapped his arm again, conveying a strange camaraderie. Nickie ignored Durq's cringe at her sudden amiability so soon after she'd scared the crap out of him. "You got this D-boy!"

Durq glanced over at Grim who had been trying to help shift the boxes. He was perspiring and panting, and other than a weak smile he offered their new crew member nothing more.

"We'll be back on the bridge," Nickie called, stomping out toward the corridor. She turned, beckoning Grim to hurry up. Grim picked up his feet and hurried after her. She hit some keys on the door panel, concentrating for a moment while she translated them from Skaine characters in her head. "I'm locking this door down, so they can't get access to the rest of the ship."

Durq's face dropped, bewildered, as he stood, shoulders slouched, in the middle of the cargo hold amongst the fake crates of weapons. "But…."

"You'll be fine," Nickie grinned, winking at him as the door clamped shut sealing him off and trapping him inside.

"You think he'll be ok?" Grim asked nervously.

"He's Skaine. This kind of dodgy dealing is in his blood. All he's got to do is show them the weapons and get them to hand over the money. Then we've got them."

"And then we rain all hell down on them?"

"See, Grim'Zee? You're getting it," she said, patting him on the back before striding off down the corridor back to the bridge.

CHAPTER SIX

Bates residence, Spire, Estaria

Carol and Philip sat in their dining room eating take-out food that Carol had ordered in on her way home. Either of them finding time to cook was nigh-on impossible since Philip had come back out of retirement. Plus, the responsibilities of running an off-book spy department also meant that dinners turned into debriefings.

"I talked with Arlene today," Carol told Philip as she took another sip of the micronutrient enhanced wine he'd bought a case of before he went back to work.

He finished chewing. "Well, that was bound to happen at some point."

"It was," she agreed.

"And? Everything ok?"

"Yes. Fine. She wanted me to look into something. That trouble that Molly's been having with the university. Sounds like they're running out of options."

"Ahhh. And they need your help now."

"Sounds like."

Philip looked amused. She never could understand why he

was so uninvested in the social politics that made up a big part of their role as a department, and as individual operatives. "So what did they want? The loan of a wily assassin? Intel on a shady politician?"

"Well, yes... and no," she demurred, putting her knife and folk down. "I think they want it to be managed quietly but without killing anyone."

Philip tutted. "Do-gooders."

"I know," she agreed, rolling her eyes.

"So what? You going to put an agent on it?"

"Well, I wondered if it would be a good test for your protege—"

Philip barely gave her the chance to finish her sentence. "I did have a series of exercises for him." It sounded like a rejection, but his eyes lit up as if he himself had just been invited back into the field.

"Well, if you can spare him from your spy craft training shenanigans, you can have him back after he's done."

"What do you need him to do?"

"Find out where the order came from for the review on the university... and then use leverage to overturn the order." Carol started eating again.

Philip nodded. "Any other constraints?"

She paused for a moment. "Yes. Try to make sure it doesn't cost me an arm and a leg."

"Ok, so no buying people. Got it." Philip grinned. "Bribery is only effective in about forty-six percent of cases anyway," he muttered knowingly. "There are many more ways to persuade people to change their minds."

Carol sniggered quietly. "And no violence. This will get back to our daughter one way or another. They're all so... friendly down there." She made a face. "No way Arlene would keep a secret like that from her."

"Fine," Philip agreed nonchalantly. "No violence, no killing, no bribing. I'll just have to tell Hans that his hands are tied."

"Was that a misplaced torture pun?" his wife asked, one eyebrow raised.

Philip looked sheepish. "Yeah. It sounded better in my head," he confessed as he went back to munching the remains of food on his plate.

Aboard *The Empress*, Agresh Quadrant

"We're going to need weapons and suits," Sean told her as he strode to a cabinet on the front wall. She followed. He opened the cabinet to reveal an array of weapons and gear, from protection equipment and space suits, down to gloves and accessories.

Karina whistled. "Wow. Some supply cabinet."

Sean gave her a flirtatious look. "This is nothing. Wait till I show you round the warehouse we have on the base."

She smiled seductively back at him. "I'll look forward to it."

He caught the glint in her eye and pretended to be occupied with the mission, handing her a blast-proof vest. "Put this on," he told her.

He moved down the row of weapons and selected out one thing after another: pistols for legs, ankles, assault blasters, laser rifles. Guided deployment scopes. One item after another they geared themselves up and in a matter of minutes, they were ready.

Joel appeared coming down the metal steps to the bay. "Hey. So we're clear on the mission outcomes?"

Sean grinned, heading over to a pod while strapping a device onto his wrist. "Yeah. Kill anything that moves once the exchange has happened?"

Joel rolled his eyes. Karina smiled. "Don't worry, I'll keep him in check," she promised, patting Sean on a shoulder as she followed him.

The three arrived at the two pods. "No," Joel countered, his face now serious but unemotional. "We need to do this right. We don't want any blowback from the Federation. We need to see the weapons, verify their source, and then get them to take the money. Then we can prove that they're trading arms illegally. Then unless they fire first, we want to bring them in."

Karina nodded, climbing into the first pod. Sean sighed. "Man, you really know how to make this boring," he teased.

Joel didn't budge. "Do it right, Royale. Molly doesn't need the heat on this one."

Sean's expression softened. "Yeah. Ok," he agreed, closing the door to his pod.

Joel stepped back allowing the pair the space to take off.

Inside the Pod, Sean connected to Karina. "You heard him. We'll do this by their book, yeah?"

Karina glanced at him through the side window. "That was the plan all along, honey."

Sean exhaled sharply in pretend frustration. "Ok. Emma?"

"Here. Preparing to transfer," Emma responded.

"Good. Take us out."

The cargo doors opened, revealing the forcefield which would allow them out, but not the air or anything else in the hold.

Joel took another couple of steps back out of the way as the two pods gently lifted off and headed gently out into the nothingness of space. He waited for the doors to start closing and then started walking back up to the steps and back to the cockpit.

It was a matter of minutes that they were in space between the two ships.

"Ok, their cargo doors are opening," Sean reported over the pod audio feed. "Are we sure their forcefield is modulated for safe passage?"

"Affirmative," Emma responded. "I've checked it out. We're good. Preparing to breach and land."

Karina watched from the second pod, just a short distance

behind Sean as the pods came in to descend through the opening door. A few moments later Sean's pod passed through the yellowish film and set down gently on the cargo hold floor. Her pod continued straight after as if in a mechanized sequence. She felt quite out of control as it lurched forward automatically.

Sean was already getting out of his pod as her pod settled probably less than a foot above the floor. She hit the button and undid the press stud on her right legged firearm. Just in case, she told herself.

Sean was already talking with the Skaine. "You speak good Federation!" she could hear him saying. He turned to introduce her. "This is Karina."

Karina immediately thought it was strange that he was passing pleasantries with the Skaine. She hopped down and moved toward the pair so she could hear better what was happening.

"Nice to meet you," the Skaine responded. "I'm Durq."

Sean and Karina exchanged confused glances.

Durq stood awkwardly for a moment. "I suppose you want to see the weapons then?" he said, suddenly remembering the script.

"Yes, please," Sean agreed.

Durq headed over to the crate that Nickie had carefully left out and half open for him. "Here we go," he said, pulling the lid fully off.

Sean edged forward to inspect the cargo.

Aboard *The Empress*, Agresh Quadrant

"Erm, Crash? I do believe we have a problem." Emma's voice sounded through the cockpit of the Empress.

"Go ahead," Crash responded, in his distinctive pilot's tonality.

"It seems that we're not dealing with Skaines at all."

"But that is definitely a Skaine ship they just boarded?"

"Yes. I've managed to tap into their security camera feed. It seems that it's being run by a human and a Yollin up on the bridge."

Crash flicked a few switches to see what visual he could get from the outside of the ship. He turned to Brock. "We need Molly back up here stat."

Brock flipped his holo open and connected a call to her. "She's on her way.'

"Can we get anything on screen?" Crash asked Emma.

"Yes, I'm having a hard time getting a real-time feed, but Oz has just started grabbing a segment of recorded footage."

The sound of boots clomping up the stairs to the cockpit distracted him for a moment. Molly appeared, closely followed by Joel.

"What've we got?" she asked, immediately leaning over Crash's shoulder to see what was going on. Just then Emma managed to display the footage on the main screen. Molly straightened up to watch it.

It showed a Yollin and a human arriving in the cockpit of the ship.

Not a Skaine in sight.

Molly cocked her head. "Emma? Any chance we could get footage from the time we had the communication with them?"

"Working on it now."

Joel stepped around Molly to get a better look at the screen. "What are we thinking? That they're using a Skaine front to get a higher price? Or prevent people taking advantage of them?"

Molly pulled her lips to one side. "Yeah. I think maybe... But why would a human and a Yollin be teamed up, out in the middle of nowhere? And why in a Skaine ship? And how come they're not dead already if they stole that ship? And why go up against Leath? I mean, there must be easier sales they could make... Less risky options."

Pieter lifted his head from his collection of holos he had been working on in the back of the cockpit. "Unless it's all a ruse?"

"For what end, though?" Joel asked.

Pieter shrugged. "We won't know until we have all the pieces."

Molly turned back to Crash. "Think we can get Sean a carefully worded message to let him know that there isn't a ship full of Skaines?"

Crash nodded and relayed the message, choosing his wording carefully so as not to miscommunicate. Sean wouldn't be able to respond if he were in the middle of the exchange.

"Sean, listen carefully but try not to respond until we have a plan. I'm here with Molly. We've noticed that the Skaine in front of you is likely the only Skaine on the ship. We have two other life signals in the cockpit. One human. One Yollin."

There was quiet on the line.

Sean had zoned out holding a Zorg ZF-1 weapon, half-cocked. He glanced over at Karina, wondering how he could relay the intel. Then he saw a nervous flicker in her eyes as she glanced back, and could tell from her expression she had gotten the same message.

Good. That made things easier.

Crash's voice continued. "Can you let me know you understand?"

Sean smiled at the Skaine and flipped the weapon onto its other side as he held it in his arms. "I understand..." he paused, "that there are custom-made versions of these available in some markets."

"Yes. I guess," the Skaine responded. "But I wouldn't know much about that."

Back on the ship Molly heard the response. She stood straight and folded her arms, thinking. "Ok. So now we have to figure out how to play this out. It's a delicate situation, we want to tread softly. One wrong move and we risk an inter-species diplomatic crisis, and I don't want Lance riding me for that as well as everything el—"

Her eye caught the monitor again. Sean flipped the weapon back into his normal firing arm and was pointing it at the Skaine. "You wanna tell me what's really going on here, then?" he demanded, stepping forward toward the terrified Skaine. "Before I blow your brains out?"

His words filled the cockpit on *The Empress*.

Molly's head dropped into one of her hands, hiding her face.

Joel shrugged, nonchalantly. "Guess that's 'treading softly' gone out of the window."

Brock and Pieter snorted quietly from the corner.

Clandestine Location #1

The Sark had been up for only a matter of an hour or so. Hans Duo walked briskly hunched against the biting cold of the morning. He had precise instructions for meeting his handler. Well, he assumed it was his handler at least. The coded message was from an unknown source, so technically he could be being summoned by anyone.

Odds were it was Philip.

He was way too enthusiastic about this spycraft stuff.

He had a code phrase to utter when he was approached. The subtext of the message had indicated that the person he was meeting knew what he looked like. He was instructed to wait ten yards down from the river monument and to make sure he wasn't followed.

It could be a test, to make sure he was running anti-surveillance protocols. That's why when he left his home in the morning he'd changed his mode of transport twice, and directions three times. He wasn't going to fail this if it was a test. And he definitely wasn't going to mess things up if was a real op.

He'd just done a lap of the lake to make sure that there wasn't anything suspicious, but it was time he was at the monument. He broke into a jog, musing to himself that at least with all this exercise he could probably skip PT later.

He arrived at the meeting point and looked around. He noticed a young woman with a baby in a stroller. It was early for a young mom to be out like this. Especially if she didn't have to be at work. He looked for any other signs. There was a mocha stand a few hundred feet away, just back from the river that came through the park. It seemed like a hive of activity for anyone suited and booted who came through the park. There was a homeless person on a bench a hundred feet to his left. And a couple of joggers he'd already seen on his walk. Nothing out of place yet.

He kept his awareness all around him. And then decided that if he needed to wait much longer he was going to have to grab a mocha in order to look less suspicious, of course.

Just then he heard someone behind him. "The Estarian flag is flying upside down today," a familiar voice said.

Hans relaxed. He could smell mocha. His meeting had brought the mochas. And managed to approach without Hans detecting him. "It's a fine day for a rally," he responded, before slowly turning to face his mentor and handler.

Philip grinned, as if excited that Hans managed to get it right. He handed him the mocha. "Greetings of the day upon you," he said. "Obviously if this were a real meet we'd be acting like we didn't know each other."

Hans took the mocha. "Obviously," he agreed.

Philip took a sip of his mocha, then indicated they should walk. The pair ambled alongside the river.

"So, did I pass?" Hans asked.

"Were you followed?"

"I don't think so."

"Well, then you did."

67

ELL LEIGH CLARKE & MICHAEL ANDERLE

Hans thought this was too simple for one of Philip's usual tests. "What am I missing?"

Philip chuckled lightly. "Ah. You're onto me. Good." He paused, looking out over the park as if admiring the beauty of the morning. "I have a job for you. Something that will tell us how your skills are coming along."

"You mean a test?"

"Yeah, something like that. Live case though. You think you're up to it."

"This is what I was born for."

Philip smiled at the enthusiasm. He reminded him of himself when he was a new agent. "Ok, here are the details," he said, bumming a file over to Hans's holo. "We need these people to remove their pressure on the Health and Safety department and get them to retract the findings of the investigation on the university."

Hans glanced down to see the file had uploaded. He continued to stroll casually, drinking his mocha. "This is to do with the university investigation and shut down?"

"One and the same."

"Force permitted?"

"I would prefer a more sophisticated approach. Let this be a test of finesse."

Hans smirked over his paper cup. "Director Bates told you no force, didn't she?"

Philip sighed. "Yes. And no bribes. And no killing."

"Tying our hands," Hans smiled dryly.

"From the mouths of babes," Philip chuckled. "Yes. But also, I suspect it's a little more nuanced than that. This is associated with Molly's institution. Having been a part of it, you know what they stand for. You know why you went there."

"And really, it's how I feel," Hans stated flatly.

"Right."

"I wasn't joking."

"Course you were, son."

"No. I wasn't. I wouldn't take someone out as a first option."

Philip bobbed his head. "Well, okay then. Anyway, if you know anything about this, you'll know that we're on a tight timescale to make this go away. Run any moves past me before you make them, and make sure you're not compromised in any way. Remember, this is the reputation of the institution on the line. The future of the work they do."

"I understand, Sir. I'll keep you in the loop."

"Good. Ok. I'll see you back at the office. You take the south exit. I'll double back and use the central gate."

"Ok, sir." Hans raised his mocha cup as a thank you, and the two parted company to continue with the official part of their days.

CHAPTER SEVEN

Special Task Force Offices, Undisclosed location, Estaria

Alisha rocked on her console chair, flicking between lines of data on two different screens.

"I got something," Joshua announced over the group holo connection they'd left open since the morning meeting.

Alisha finished scanning to a point where she could stop and put a marker on her place. "What is it?" she asked, glad of the distraction.

"There's a statement in the city hall archives. A landlord reported a resident disappearing, without packing up his stuff or giving notice."

Alisha wasn't getting it.

"Why is that odd?" Rhodez asked over the audio feed, swivelling around in his console chair across the aisle to look at his teammates.

"It's odd because the resident was one Mr. Robert Califray."

"Wait," Alisha flicked to her notes on her other screen. "That's Beaufort's former undersecretary."

"It is," Joshua confirmed, winking at Alisha. "Checked the address and date of birth. All seems legit. Except for the part where he seems to have just disappeared. No more banking transactions. No holo calls. Everything that is on an auto pay just keeps going out. No family seems to be stepping in and running his estate. No missing person's report. Just the complaint about the rent not being paid and the court's ruling that the items could be auctioned off and removed."

"Shit," Alisha hissed under her breath. "How come no one's reported him missing?"

"Phone records seem to show he didn't have any regular contact with any family." Joshua flicked a few screens, "But then, it also looks like they just assumed he'd skipped town. They tried to reach him on his holo and he didn't respond."

"What did they say at his place of work?" Rhodez asked. He had shuffled off his console chair and was heading over to talk to the team in person.

Josh shrugged. "No report filed."

Alisha was already on her feet. "I think we need to pay our Senator a visit."

"You guys go ahead," Rhodez told them. "I'm doing some digging on the previous occupant of the other position that magically got filled on Thursday."

"Houston."

"Yeah. Malone Houston was the previous guy."

"Cool. We'll keep you posted," Joshua promised.

Rhodez ambled off back toward his console. "Hey, Grab me a bagel on your way back in!"

"Cheese and chicken?"

"Yeah! With extra chilies please."

"Consider it done." Joshua patted Rhodez on his shoulder as he headed in the other direction toward the door.

Alisha trotted out after him, pulling her atmojacket on as she walked.

· · ·

Beaufort's office, Senate House, Spire

"So, what can the Department of Near Space Communications do for Spire's finest?" Beaufort stepped forward to shake the hands of the two detectives presenting themselves in his office. His slick suit and hair full of product gave him an impeccable if not overly-polished, appearance.

Joshua and Alisha shook the hand of Senator Garet Beaufort and then put away their cover ids. No investigation warranted telling their targets that they were a secret off-shoot of Estaria's Clandestine services.

"We're looking into the disappearance of your former employee. Robert Califray," Joshua told him.

"Robert? I heard he went on holiday and decided not to come back."

Alisha nodded. "We think that story was fabricated. We can't find any record of him communicating that back to anyone here." She paused. "How did your office receive notification of this?"

Garet shrugged and walked around his desk to sit down. "I have no idea. Hang on." He pressed a button on his desk. "Diana, can you come in here please."

"Yes, sir," the intercom returned.

"Diana is the most likely to know," he explained. "She keeps my schedule like it was a military operation, but she's also tapped into the water cooler, as it were."

The door opened and the assistant who had let them in appeared in the room. "Yes, sir?"

"Diana, can you tell these folks how we came to find out about Robert leaving us?"

Diana thought for a moment. "Well, after a couple of days of him not showing up for work after his vacation I think his assistant tried contacting him on his holo. He didn't get any response, he went to his apartment. Landlord said something about the rent being due and that he was going to file proceedings."

"And then what?"

"And then a few days later we received a communication from Robert's holo saying that he realized some things on his vacation and that he wouldn't be coming back to town."

"Anything else you remember?"

Diana shook her head. "You should probably talk to his assistant though. She'll be able to tell you more."

"Great. Let's do that now," Alisha suggested. "Can you introduce us?"

"Sure." Diana led the way from the room, leaving Garet and Joshua alone.

"So... sounds a bit suspicious," Garet said, "now that you guys have shown up."

"You didn't think it was odd at the time?"

"Oh of course, but what are you going to do. The guy told them that he was done with us, so we just took it at face value."

Joshua watched and waited. His training had told him to speak only up to twenty percent of the time, and that his interviewee would fill the gaps...and end up saying more than he had intended.

Garet wiped the bottom half of his face. "You know... the thing that wasn't widely known was that we heard that he had just got out of a bad relationship. I guess Diana was trying to spare him the humiliation just now. But I heard it ended very badly and the vacation was his way of resetting."

Joshua nodded. "Understandable. You think it hit him hard?"

"Undoubtedly. He was different. I mean, he was never a singing-in-the-hills kinda guy, but he turned more morose and snapped at a few people before he left. Someone even mentioned that he had alcohol on his breath in a meeting the week before."

"Hmm. Interesting."

"So you're thinking it was personal problems that made him run off?"

"We're still considering all the options," Joshua told him. "But

ELL LEIGH CLARKE & MICHAEL ANDERLE

this has been very helpful." Joshua stood up to go, but then he turned back to the senator.

"You don't happen to know where he went on vacation, do you?"

Garet shook his head. "I'm not sure. Somewhere off-world, I think. Diana will probably know though."

"Ok. I'll find out. Thanks very much for your time Mr. Beaufort."

"Of course," he replied politely, getting up from his desk and walking the detective out. "And if there is anything else we can help with, please don't hesitate."

The two men shook hands, and Joshua headed out into the reception area of Garet's office.

Just then the assistant returned. "Your colleague is just in the next office," she told him helpfully.

"Thanks, Diana. Appreciate it."

Joshua stalked out of the office with a casual wave and headed one door down. Alisha was just finishing up and the two emerged a few moments later together.

"So, find out anything interesting?" Alisha asked.

Joshua gave her a tight smile. "Not here," he told her quietly, opening the corridor door for her and following her out.

Back out on the sidewalk away from other employees, they stood along the side of the building. "So you think it's been made to look like there were personal reasons?" she asked.

"Yeah. Either that or our assassin was an opportunist. What about you? Any thoughts from the assistant?"

"Not really. She seemed genuinely concerned about him until she received the message."

"And we're thinking that the message was bogus."

"Yeah. I'd say so... which is why I had her upload me a copy, complete with the tracking file."

"Great. Let's get that back to the team and see if we can pull a location of origin off it."

Alisha nodded. "I'm not hopeful. If it was a few days since the girl went to the apartment, arousing suspicion, he would have had a few days to figure out how to send it without it being traceable."

"That's true. Or at least making it look like it came from the vacation spot."

"Which was on Ogg, apparently," she added.

"Hmm. Well, let's just hope that our tech-fu is better than our suspect's."

"I'm sure it is. For Cleavon, it's all a matter of personal pride."

"Think you can get him to help then?"

Alisha grinned as they started walking back toward their government-issued space car. "I revert to my previous statement."

Joshua chuckled as they headed off.

CHAPTER EIGHT

Aboard *The Empress*, Agresh Quadrant

Jack appeared in the cockpit. "Emma just looped me in," she announced, her face looking several times more concerned than Brock and Pieter. "Do I need to get down there and back Sean up?"

Molly shook her head, her eyes still fixed on the screen showing the standoff. "No, not yet. Let's try the grown-up approach and talk to this human and Yollin. They're obviously pulling some kind of con."

Jack sucked air in through her teeth. "Sounds like they have a death wish. I mean, who the fuck bombs around in a Skaine ship? I imagine it's like having a target on your back."

Molly pressed her lips together. "Yeah. That's what we need to try and find out. I wonder if that's the point? Why would anyone want people to think they were Skaines unless there were certain things available to you if people thought you were Skaines. Like, you're less likely to double-cross them in a deal."

Jack frowned, her arms folded in the same posture as Molly. "You think they're riding the Skaine coat-tails just to make a quick buck?"

Molly shrugged. "Maybe. Emma, can we connect up with them?"

"Hailing them now."

Molly, there's something else. I'm finding strange patterns in the system.

You hacked in?

Yes. But... there's something...

What?

I'm not sure. Standby.

"Ok, they're responding," Emma announced.

The Skaine voice started again over the audio feed into the cockpit. The translation appeared on the screen again. "Are you ready to transfer the funds?"

"Emma, put me through, in standard Federation."

"Opening two-way audio."

Molly cleared her throat and spoke as clearly as she could. "Yes. In a moment," she said slowly. "I just need to understand why you're going to the trouble of speaking to me in Skaine when actually you're human."

There was a muttering on the line, and some scuffling.

Then a long pause.

"Hello?" Molly pressed.

"Yes, hello," a sulky female human voice responded. "Well, it sounds like you're also human. So I dunno what you're complaining about."

"I am. But why are you pretending to be Skaine?"

"Why are you pretending to be Leath?" the human female shot back.

"I'm out to catch some bad guys," Molly retorted.

"As am I."

"Who are you?"

There was another pause.

"Ranger Two," the girl responded, with a little more attitude than was really necessary.

Molly hit the mute button on the panel in front of Crash. "Oz? What is Ranger Two?"

Sean chirped up over the feed. "I can tell you who Ranger Two is, and that wasn't her voice. It's an impostor."

Molly frowned. "What? How do you know?"

"Trust me. Long story, but I know," he said cryptically. Molly could see he was still holding the Skaine at gunpoint. "Can we get on with blowing these impostors up? My arms are getting tired."

Karina's voice came over the channel. "You're out of condition honey. More gym practice for you..."

Sean grunted and responded with something Molly didn't want to hear. She clamped her hands over her ears. "All right, you two! Get a room!"

She muted Sean and Karina and unmuted her connection with the Skaine cockpit. "I have it on good authority that you are not Ranger Two. So where does that leave us?"

Aboard *The Penitent Granddaughter*, Agresh Quadrant

"Shit, fuck, wank!"

Nickie hit the mute button in the cockpit.

"What is it?" Grim asked, now looking even more anxious than had they been actual Leath on the other end of the deal.

"They can only know that I'm not the real Ranger Two if they knew Aunt Tabitha...and the chances of that are pretty slim, since she left this part of the galaxy a loooong time ago."

"Wait, what? So, you stole your Aunt's Ranger badge?"

"No. Of course not," Nickie rolled her eyes. "Not even close..." She started pacing, "Think, Nickie. *Think. Think. Think...* And Meredith, you can jump in and help any time soon."

Meredith's voice came over the cockpit audio for them both to hear. "Well, my initial course of action would be not killing them. It would be prudent since they are on a Federation ship and so automatically presumed friend rather than foe."

Nickie continued to pace. "Don't you have some kind of uplink that could tell us who they are?" she asked. "Couldn't you have seen this coming?"

"I'm afraid not. I have very limited connection with the Federation here, and what connection I do have cannot transmit the kind of data I'd need to—"

"Okay, okay. Not useful at the moment." She paused. "So it seems the real solution is to hotfoot it out of here. If the Federation catches me impersonating a Ranger…"

"Well technically," Meredith continued over the cockpit's intercom, "the Rangers are disbanded, so that's a gray area that might get off on a technicality. The other thing is you now have two of their personnel on board."

"Fuck. *Shit!* Fucking… Just *Fuck!*"

Grim chirped up. "I see the Tourette's medication is wearing off."

"I'll say. I'll be ready for a proper drink when this is over. If even Meredith is basically saying that we're screwed, then we're scre—"

Meredith interjected, "I said no such thing. If anything, I see you have an opportunity. Aren't you at least curious as to who these people are? And how they know your aunt?"

"Well, yes, of course I'm curious. But I also can't get caught. There's no way I'm coming back in from the cold right now."

Meredith made a tutting sound. "No one says you need to, Nickie. You could just meet with them and gather more information. Find out what you need to know, and then get back to chasing down **Skaine**s."

Nickie paused. "What's their weapons status?"

"They have them. Fully functioning. But they're not locked on."

She continued pacing. "So, no imminent threat?"

"No imminent threat."

Nickie's pacing slowed. "And we do have two of their people."

"You do."

Nickie stopped dead. "Maybe it's time to have a chat with them..."

Grim was on his feet again. "Wait what does that mean? What are you going to do?"

But Nickie was already heading out of the door with a purpose he'd only seen once before... when they were under fire from a ship full of Skaines trying to kill them.

Oz cracked through another layer of the Federation security on the processor that seemed to be controlling the Skaine ship.

"Well, hello. What have we here?" He wondered. He ran a signal through one of the input nodes that he had managed to disconnect, and it shut down and ran a signal back via the same message stream.

"Federation software. No doubt about that. But you're pretty damn fast at reacting."

Yes, I am, a message shot back.

Too fast to be just a standalone program, Oz thought to himself.

Something tells me that you're far more sophisticated. And not of human origin.

You'd be correct in that assumption. But you're not constructed like anything I've ever seen either.

You're a Federation EI like Emma, and Scamp?

I have no idea who Emma is, but Scamp...Scamp I know. The EI that runs the Scamp Princess.

Yes. That's right. The Queen Bitch's secret vessel.

So Scamp is still around?

That's correct. And you said 'still'. So what? Are you from the past? Or from the Federation from a long time ago.

Yes. Both. May I be frank?

You can call yourself anything you like. I'm Oz.

Hello, Oz. But I meant "frank," as in "candid."

I know. I was making a joke.

Oh. I see.

Oz mused to himself how tedious EIs were when they hadn't installed his humor upgrade patch.

Since we are both from the Federation, I think it's safe to say that we are probably both on the same team.

Yes. That is a logical conclusion.

Well then, I think I can share information with you that will mean that we no longer have to keep up pretenses and we may even be able to bring our humans together.

Sounds like a plan. So what's really going on here?

Aboard *The Empress*, Agresh Quadrant

Molly, I think you ought to know. that the situation is evolving. Rapidly.

Molly stood still watching the main screen in the cockpit.

You're telling me. The girl just left the cockpit. I suspect she's heading down to the cargo bay which means she might be planning to space Sean and Karina. Something tells me that she doesn't like being fooled.

Well, I have information that may put a stop to that. Meredith is working on that now.

Meredith?

Yep. Nickie's EI.

Nickie? The girl? You're on first name terms with the enemy now?

Yes. But they're not the enemy. It seems that we've all got our wires crossed.

Oh, you think?

That was sarcasm, wasn't it?

Like you need to check.

Well anyway. Yes. We've both been going after the same exchange. Nickie and Meredith were trying to impersonate the Skaines and meet with the Leath and we were trying to meet with the Skaines. Somehow in amongst everything we managed to intercept each other, rather than the *actual* bad guys.

Molly had been standing quietly in the middle of the cockpit. Joel had twigged that she and Oz were talking, from the changing microexpressions on her face. Only now when her breathing returned to normal did he reach out from the console chair he was occupying and swat her hand, bringing her back to the outside world.

"What's going on?" he asked.

"It would appear that our friends out there, are actually our friends. Federation no less. They were going after the same exchange we were."

There was a muttering from Brock and Pieter as they heard the news.

What do you want to do?

I don't know yet. Let me think. Tell Sean and Karina to stand by.

Spy offices, Spire

Joshua and Alisha strode through the underground office, between the two banks of console chairs occupied by their former classmates. Alisha carried three smoothies in a carrier. Joshua swung a paper bag of delicious-smelling bakery products by his side.

They arrived at their consoles and sat down on the normal non-console chairs at the table between their workstations.

Alisha set the drinks down and took them from their holder. "Where's Rhodez?"

"Don't worry," Joshua teased, opening the bag of bagels. "As soon as he gets a whiff of these bad boys he'll appear."

Alisha giggled. "Ok. Gimme two minutes I just wanna get this over to Cleavon." She got up and scooted around the back of Joshua's console, pulling up her holo as she walked.

Just then Rhodez appeared. "Joshua, my man. Good job!"

Joshua handed the bagel over along with a side of fries. "Figured you'd need the extra calories," he chuckled. Rhodez slapped his sides. "Of course. Need to keep this machine fueled!"

"Where did Alisha go?"

"She's seeing if Cleavon can help us out with a trace. Looks like our guy sent a message saying he was leaving town for good... only after people started digging around into his whereabouts."

Rhodez frowned. "From your presentation of the facts am I to assume we're thinking foul play at this point?"

"That's what I'm hoping Cleavon will confirm. And you know, a point of origin would be helpful too."

Rhodez pulled up a guest seat by his team's shared desk and started unpacking his lunch, savoring the divine scent of the bagel as if he hadn't eaten in a week.

A playful smile touched Joshua's lips as he watched him with amusement, taking his time to get his own bagel unwrapped.

Alisha returned to her console. "Ok. Our tech-fu master is all over it. Told him that there's an evening of drinks in it if he can get us the result sooner rather than later." She sat down, reaching over Joshua to grab her own food, and shifting the shakes around so they each had the correct one.

"Did you manage to find anything useful?" she asked Rhodez.

He had just bitten into his bagel and his eyes conveyed his utter dismay that she should interrupt his sacred bagel experience with a work question. He pointed at his mouth and chewed deliberately showing he wasn't just ignoring her.

Eventually he finished and swallowed. "Ok, so it looks like our guy over at the Department of Off-World Logistics got ousted for embezzlement. On first glance, everything looks in order. Closer inspection revealed payments going into his account from an off-planet account which we suspect is dodgy. All picked up in a routine spot check."

Alisha frowned, chewing slowly.

"You're right to be suspicious," Rhodez continued. "It seems that these deposits were coming into the same account the government pays his money into. If he hadn't done that he could have kept the off-planet account isolated and undetected." He wiped some mustard off the table with a napkin and screwed it up.

"Can we tie him to the off-planet account otherwise?"

Rhodez shook his head. "Don't think so. I've been trying... but other than those payments, that other account could belong to anyone from my Aunt Bessy to a crime syndicate."

"Curiouser and curiouser," Joshua muttered. "So you're thinking he was framed?"

"Yeah. Apparently, he protested he was when he was first interviewed, and then somewhere during the eight-week-long investigation he changed his story."

Joshua's face scrunched up. "Who wants to bet that he was either paid off or threatened to cop to it?"

Alisha was chewing and raised her hand to vote, dropping bits of salad in the bagel wrapper.

Rhodez continued. "After lunch, I'm gonna head over there and have a chat with our so-called embezzler and see if I can find any links to chase up the chain. The threat must have come from someone."

Joshua clicked his fingers. "Cool. So you're going to try and get him to tell you and not try and force the issue on whether he was telling the truth about the money?"

"Yeah. Of course." He gave Joshua a sideways glance. "I gradu-ated the same courses you did, *stom kop*!" Joshua bobbed his head rhythmically feeling a little embarrassed.

Rhodez didn't dwell on it though. "If we can get those guys into custody then maybe there's a chance of having the results of the first investigation overturned, and he won't have a chance to go back on the very thing he's been forced to declare."

Alisha snorted lightly. "Ha! Good luck with that. If someone's been forced to give up their livelihood they're not likely to tell who forced them."

Rhodez grinned at her, finishing his bagel. "That sounds like a challenge to me. Care to offer a wager?"

Alisha chuckled. "Same deal as Clevedon?"

"You're on!"

The athletic Estarian scooted up from his seat and screwed up his wrapper and grabbed the shake. "Thanks for lunch folks. My turn next time." He winked, and with that he strode back to his desk to grab his jacket and bounce the address onto his holo.

Cleavon appeared by Joshua's elbow, getting Alisha's attention. "I've managed to track down an address. At this point, given the tech he's using, which was probably developed either in the same labs we get our gear from... or possibly the Federation... anyway, with the tools I have I've nailed it down to a location. It's mid-town."

"You mean here in Spire?" she clarified, her bagel hovering forgotten between its wrapper and her mouth.

"Yeah."

Joshua glanced at Alisha, gauging her reaction to the information.

"Great," she said, marginally distracted by Joshua. "Wanna bounce it over to me? We'll go check it out when we're done here."

"Sure." Cleavon hesitated. "You know, I'd... if I didn't have so much do for Charlie team I'd offer to come with you. You know, run it down and all. See the job through."

Alisha opened her mouth to speak.

"It's all right buddy," Joshua jumped in. "We've got it. Your team needs you here."

ELL LEIGH CLARKE & MICHAEL ANDERLE

"But hey," Alisha added, "we totally appreciate your help. I said you were the best man for the job."

Cleavon blushed a little, his starched collar seeming a little tighter than when he dressed that morning. He tugged at it. "Good. So, um. When this pans out... we're on for drinks at The Constable, right?"

Alisha flashed her best smile, comfortable to be back in the realms of their mercenary exchange. "Yes. Absolutely." She winked. "Your kung-fu has to be better than the perp's though, else you lose!"

Cleavon relaxed and started walking away, waving as he did. It was almost as if his confidence rematerialized as soon as they were talking about their bet. "Run it down. You'll see!"

Alisha chuckled.

Joshua waited until he was out of earshot before leaning forward over the table, missing an errant mustard blob by a fraction of an inch. "Someone has a crush on you!"

Alisha grabbed a napkin and cleaned her hands dismissively. "Don't be silly. It's Cleavon. He just likes a challenge."

"Yes, but I think we're disagreeing about the type of challenge!"

Alisha rolled her eyes. "Have you finished? We should get going so we have something to report to the Director at the evening debrief."

Joshua screwed up his empty wrapper. "I'm ready."

Alisha folded the remainder of her bagel up and shoved it into her bottom drawer. "Good. I need two minutes to wash up."

CHAPTER NINE

Clandestine Location #2

The city was alive with activity. It would make a good cover, and easier to slip away if they were being watched. But Hans had decided to mix the game up a little. After all, if Philip did insist on doing these briefings as a way of refining their skills then they should stretch their imaginations too.

He only hoped that Philip had managed to decode the time and location he had sent him via an old-fashioned paper note. Things were different since his day and Hans had been becoming increasingly aware of how differently the two generations processed information. He hoped that the awareness was going to be enough for him to manage to work with others in the field when he needed to.

He thought briefly about the teams and the bonds that were forming between the members of the task force. In some ways he envied them. But out here, on his own? *That* was where the real action and opportunities lay. His loneliness was a small sacrifice to make.

He peeked around the corner of the big concrete block in the car park. He hoped that Philip knew the building as well as he

ELL LEIGH CLARKE & MICHAEL ANDERLE

gave the impression that he had. Hans had been trying to work out all the blind spots in the cameras since day one: since they told him that kind of knowledge was important for an operative.

He heard footsteps. Two sets. Footsteps that were making absolutely no attempt to stay quiet. It was probably someone else. He heard a female laugh, and a male's voice. It was Alisha and Joshua. He waited, listening. A car door opened. Then the other. They both closed, and the engine started up. He listened to the sound of them driving away.

He was about to peek around the column again when a sound to his left pulled his attention. He looked around, and there was Philip! Making an approach without Hans detecting him, again.

Dammit, he thought to himself. He had felt sure he would make him this time.

Philip smiled. "Good spot." He looked up and pointed with his eyes at the two cameras they had avoided.

Hans sighed and stood up from the column. "I had been trying to make sure I could see you coming," he confessed.

"Ah, don't take it so hard. I've been a spook longer than you've been alive," Philip told him. "Sometimes there's no substitute for experience."

Hans didn't feel any better, but he nodded and moved on anyway. "I've made some progress on the assignment," he told his handler. "It seems that their pressure is coming from two individuals. One I've already taken care of, but I needed the okay from the university for the other."

He offered his holoscreen for Philip to skim. He nodded as he eyes quickly took in the intel, catching him up to the situation.

"Cunning," he said after a few moments. "I like the way you handled the first situation. Very resourceful. How did you ensure that the agreement would go through?"

"I called the contact at the government, pretended to be an old school friend, and said that the request was coming from higher up and not to ask too many questions. Then I hacked the system and gave the employee a small pay rise to coincide with them fulfilling the request."

"Very resourceful. And untraceable?"

"Absolutely."

"Excellent. Okay, report both these to the Director when you go back upstairs, and make sure that they are on board with the other request before you grant it. Frame it as if it's a fait accompli though… no point giving them a reason to undo it."

Hans smirked. He realized that Philip was actually a lot smarter than he appeared. Hans understood the way that team dynamics worked, how people with different ideas and agendas could unravel a carefully thought out plan in a matter of minutes.

"Yes, sir," he confirmed.

"Ok, and one last thing, Hans. You managed to get to this spot, but you were seen coming here on camera. See if you can get back to the office without your path being traced. You have as long as it takes, but I'll be having one of your team pulling footage for me by end of play today."

Hans felt his stomach sink. He was so tired of this messing around when there was no real danger. He tried to keep his face straight, though. "Yes, sir."

Philip strolled off, whistling, in full view of both cameras, as casually as if he had been coming from his own car after a delightful lunch break.

Hans leaned back against his concrete column and growled quietly to himself as he wracked his brains.

So much for forcing them to be more creative, he figured.

Heddon Mocha Shop, Midtown, Spire

"This is it," Alisha said, double checking the number on the door. "A mocha shop."

Joshua looked up at the signage. "It's an ideal public place to disguise the sender of the message, it'd be impossible to know who sent it even if we did manage to pinpoint the place of origin."

Alisha leaned on the old-fashioned door plate and pushed it forward, allowing Joshua to stalk in ahead of her. "Age before beauty," she teased.

Joshua made a face at her as he stepped inside. His gaze flicked around the cafe, searching for clues as to the type of clientele, quickly profiling their average customer.

Alisha was the first to spot the camera in the corner. "Let's hope that's actually rigged up and not on the net."

Joshua nodded. "Yeah. If this hacker is good enough to have Cleavon unsure of himself for even a moment, he's probably wiped any images of himself."

Alisha's eyes fell on a sticker on some of the point-of-sale material. She pointed to it, quietly.

Joshua smiled. "The GRX payment system. Nice. Good to have a backup. Let's see if we can cross reference the time of the message with transactions just ahead of the time code."

Alisha plugged away at her holo.

"What can I get you?" Suddenly the pair had the full attention of the server behind the bar.

Joshua reached for his badge, but then hesitated. He pulled his wallet out of his inside pocket instead. "I'll have the mocha renaissance with cream on top. Alisha?"

She looked up, suddenly aware she was being called upon. "Oh um, just a straight mocha for me. Thanks."

Joshua completed the transaction, checking the time it was taking to put the transaction through, and for them to get their drinks and sit down.

Alisha showed him the list of transactions for their time period. They sat down, and he clocked the time again. "Ok. We're looking at three and a half minutes. Then he'll need time to log in, jump through his security protocols and then write and send the message."

Alisha was already punching away into the holoscreen on her wrist. "Ok. Sending the estimates to Cleavon. See if he can help us narrow it down. I'll also ask him to tap the camera."

Joshua nodded. "If we can pull it remotely we won't need to start flashing badges and risk tipping anyone off."

The pair drank their mochas waiting in relative quiet for Cleavon to come back to them.

"What you thinking?" Joshua asked eventually, noticing the distant look on Alisha's face as she looked out of the window.

She shrugged with one shoulder. "Nothing much. I was just wondering if we should ask to have Cleavon on our team?"

"You mean ask Bates to transfer him?"

"I guess."

Joshua pressed his lips together. "Do I detect a hint of—"

"No. You detect nothing, mister. It's just, we're asking a lot of him, and I think he's better suited to investigation than protection."

Joshua shrugged. "Well, this is only our second assignment. Who knows how the teams are gonna pan out and what we'll be tasked with in the future."

"You don't get the sense that we're better with intel than interference, then?"

Joshua took another glug of his mocha. "I'm... well. I guess you have a point."

"I'm gonna mention it in my report," Alisha told him decidedly. "They're probably looking to optimize the group anyway."

Joshua bobbed his head from side to side, conceding the point. "Maybe," he muttered, wondering if Carol Bates was going to like being told how to do her job.

Alisha's holo pinged. "He's got it!" She turned the tiny holo-projected screen so that Joshua could see it.

"We got a name?"

"Arnold Sloth," she told him. "It sounds familiar..."

"It would," Joshua confirmed. "That was the fixer. For the

smoke bombs incident, remember? The one that brought Duo into the fold."

Alisha's eyes flew wide. "You're right!" she exclaimed, excitedly. She quickly lowered her voice and leaned forward over their table. "So he's our link to the Northern clan!"

Joshua chewed his bottom lip. "Yep. That's our link." Before Alisha had time to process the implications he was up and out of his seat, pulling his jacket back on. "Looks like Cleavon came through for us."

Alisha couldn't hide her good humor. "Looks like you owe him drinks," she added, getting up.

"*I* owe him drinks?"

"Yeah, that was the deal I struck. I think he wants time to hang with the boys." She winked, then grabbed her jacket and takeout cup as she led the way out of the mocha shop.

Aboard *The Empress*, Agresh Quadrant

Molly moved toward the back of the cockpit. Joel got up and followed her.

"If they're Federation, then surely Sean and Karina will be safe?"

"You'd think. But I'm getting the sense that this person has gone off the reservation. She's out here, beyond the boundaries of Federation Space. And she just looks volatile. Don't you think?"

"I'd agree, actually. Her body language is characteristic of... well, let's put it this way. She wouldn't pass as a soldier, that's for sure."

Molly glanced back at the screen of the empty cockpit on the other ship. "Maybe we need to check in with Lance. Find out what the deal is."

Joel bobbed his head from side to side. "We could. But this is happening now. We don't know how long it will take to get a response, and once we loop him in, haven't we effectively failed."

Molly smirked. "I thought it was just me that thought like that?"

Joel shrugged. "Yeah, and you're our leader, so of course we adopt your parameters for success and failure."

Molly was amused but forced herself to stay on task. "Well, if it's just ego getting in the way, then we should reach out to him. The mission is more important at this point. Especially if Sean and Karina are in genuine danger."

"Well, hang on. Slow down. Sean and Karina can look after themselves. She's not going to space them without moving them to another part of her ship. She has the weapons in that space, and her pet Skaine."

Molly took a step forward. "Emma, show us the cargo holding again please."

The cargo holding room flicked back up on the screen. "You're right," she muttered to Joel. "So she's going to have to shoot them, or she's going to have to move them. And in that time, we can have a conversation with her and find out what the score is. If we need to, Sean will be able to immobilize her. Oz, can you communicate with Sean and Karina and let them know what we're thinking."

Sure. On it.

She turned back to Joel. "Looks like our call to the General can probably wait a little longer," she said smiling.

He put a hand on her shoulder and they returned to the front of the cockpit to stand behind Crash.

"Emma," she called out more loudly. "Patch me through to the Skaine ship again, I need to talk to..." she trailed off, trying to remember the name. "Nickie."

"Patching you through now," Emma confirmed. Molly's eyes never left the screens of the now empty cockpit of the Skaine ship, and the cargo holding area, watching like a hawk for the girl to appear somewhere again.

Director Bates' office, Special Task Force Offices, Undisclosed location, Estaria

"Okay. Is there anything else you've discovered?" Carol looked up again from her holoscreens.

Hans stood politely in front of her desk. "No, ma'am. That's everything."

She nodded sharply and went back to her work. He took that as a sign that he was dismissed. He hesitated. "Ma'am?"

She looked up again.

"Does this mean I need to report back to Agent Bates?"

Carol smiled. "The spycraft exercises in town wearing thin?"

He permitted himself a half smile. "Well, erm… if I'm honest." He didn't need to finish the sentence.

"I'll have a word with Philip," she promised. "He can get a little over-enthusiastic about the old school craft elements. In the meantime, see if Bravo team needs any assistance. I've noticed that Cleavon has been spending a lot of time doing analyses for both teams. I sense a change is needed after this case."

He nodded once. "Thank you, ma'am." He turned quietly and slipped out of her office, relieved that he wasn't required to jump through the tedious hoops of setting a spy meeting with his handler, only to tell him what he'd just told the director in a matter of minutes.

Carol waited until he had disappeared down the stairs into the bullpen before she opened her personal holo. She connected a call and waited for a response.

The call connected. "Greetings of the day to you," the responder said.

"Greetings, Arlene," Carol responded quietly and evenly. "I have news."

"That was fast."

"Well, we may not be the Federation, but we know what we're doing down here."

Arlene started to say something, but Carol was already moving on. "I've just had word from one of our agents that the root of the problem remains two-fold in terms of the two proponents."

"Uh-huh."

"There are two key influencers who pushed this forward," Carol explained. "Each for their own reasons. You were right. They think they're going to benefit from the school not existing. One had been taken care of."

Arlene drew breath quickly. "You didn't—"

Carol's voice sounded almost warm. "No. We didn't. Turns out there was a family business, sports equipment. All we needed to arrange was to have one of our assets in the district arrange to buy the school sports equipment from them for the foreseeable future."

"That sounds… simple."

"Yes, simple. But not easy. It's been handled."

"And the other?"

"That one is a little trickier. I need your help on it."

"What's the situation?"

"Well, the other influencer is backed by family money, so no such leverage. They were acting out of an ideology."

"Oh… this is going to be more difficult."

"Not quite. My agent discovered that there is a son. A son who is flunking out of Spire University and last weekend got into trouble for drugs. There's an investigation pending. We can make the charges go away, but that doesn't solve the problem of his education."

"You want me to see if we can take him at the university."

"It would seal the deal and mean you get to stay open."

There was a pause on the line while Arlene considered her

ELL LEIGH CLARKE & MICHAEL ANDERLE

response. She sighed. "I guess we can make it happen. It's a small price to pay."

"It is," Carol agreed firmly. It was clear that she didn't want to get into a discussion about ideologies, or fairness. This was a job. She'd been asked to do the impossible, and she delivered. Whatever the tensions she and Arlene had, Arlene realized she respected Carol's ability to get the job done.

"Who will reach out to the boy?" Arlene asked.

"We'll handle it. I'll have someone send over details for arranging his enrolment and you can take it from there."

"Thank you, Carol. I appreciate everything you've done. And I'm sure Molly will too."

Carol felt herself smiling. "Not a problem, Arlene. I'll let you get on," she added.

"Thanks. Bye Carol."

The call ended.

Arlene sat back in her seat, shaking her head softly.

"Everything okay?" Ben'or's voice came from the living room. She'd left the office door open so that he could hear some of it. The last thing she wanted was to shut him out of an operation he'd practically saved.

Arlene got up and wandered through. She could see he'd been working on his new wristholo while she'd been doing some work.

"Everything is going to be fine," she smiled. "Thanks to your brilliant insight."

Ben'or chuckled. "Glad I could be of assistance," he told her. "Now, how about we discuss dinner plans?"

Houston Residence, East Waterside, Outskirts of Spire

Rhodez rang the doorbell of the large house on the outskirts of town. Large and white, it stood as a reminder of how the city had sprawled to devour the old terraformed farming communities. An industrial generator from the previous century stood several hundred yards in the rear grounds of the house, the ground now arid and barren. He turned back to look at the track he'd driven up. The terrain was too unpredictable and unmapped to go antigrav around these parts, and it had felt like it had taken him forever just to get from the edge of town to here.

A uniformed marshal answered the door. Rhodez had his badge already in his hand. He knew how jumpy these marshals could be when they had someone high risk in custody. Last thing he wanted was to be reaching into his jacket pocket. "Afternoon. I'm Detective Rhodez with the 41st. I have a few questions for your ward."

The marshal eyeballed the ID for a moment and then stood aside to let the police officer in. "Down the hall, to the right."

Rhodez headed down the hallway and through into a spacious living room. The house may have been luxurious once upon a time, but now the fading wood decor and worn carpets made it feel like it's inhabitants were just making do in their existence.

An Estarian man sat in an armchair, hunched over the mocha table, fiddling with knick-knacks on the glass surface. There were remnants of tobacco on the table, as well as splashes of mocha. Rhodez concluded that he lived alone. Or at least there wasn't a woman in his life regularly. He held up his ID for the man. "I'm Detective Rhodez. Malone Houston?"

The man nodded, unsurprised to see a police officer in his home at this point. There was movement off in the kitchen. Rhodez could see another marshal through the serving hatch, moving around, checking cupboards for something.

"I'm here to get some clarity on the incident that has landed you in this predicament."

Houston snorted.

Rhodez guessed it was either contempt or sarcasm for the idea. He lowered his voice and made his way around to the other side of the mocha table to sit on the sofa, near to Houston. He leaned forward, an air of secrecy about what he was about to say. Houston allowed himself to be drawn in, his knick-knacks on the table forgotten, and his body language shifting slightly.

"Let's say you *didn't* do what you have been accused of," Rhodez started. Houston stopped for a moment. Rhodez could see he'd captured his attention for a second.

Then Houston sighed and sat back in his armchair. "I've confessed," he said simply. "That's all there is to it."

"But it's not. I know you were set up, and I know that someone has forced you to plead guilty."

Houston started to protest, but Rhodez held his hand up to silence him. "Look," Rhodez continued, still in a hushed voice. "I'm after the guys that pressured you. There's a lot more at stake than you realize. This is bigger than you, or I, and we're on the clock to stop at least two murders before they happen."

Houston's brow furrowed, as if he was contemplating helping, but he shook his head. "I can't."

Rhodez sat back, thinking. "What happened when you protested your innocence?"

Houston shrugged. "The police just kept showing me my bank statement. The more I said that I didn't know anything about the transfers, the more they insisted I did."

"And what about the account where the money came from?"

"I had never heard of the name on the account before. But they said it had been central to their investigation—and that I would have got away with it if I hadn't transferred the funds to my checking account."

"So, they were already onto the account then?"

Houston nodded.

"Sounding more and more like a set up to me." He paused. "You changed your story at one point too."

Houston shrugged. "Lawyer said it was the best way to get a reduced sentence."

Rhodez made a note on his holo. "Anything else happen

around the time you changed your story? Did they find any other evidence? Or start putting more pressure on you?"

Houston shook his head. "No. If anything they started to leave off a little. Lawyer said it was a bad sign because it meant they had something that made their case more solid."

"And that's when he pushed you to confess?"

"Yeah. He managed to get me a really good deal. Four years down from twenty."

"Really?" Rhodez had to work hard to hide his surprise and outrage. "Who told you it was twenty years on the table for embezzlement?"

"I..." he hesitated. "I think it was Scarlet?"

"Scarlet? Is that a girlfriend?"

"No. My attorney, Henry Scarlet."

Rhodez made another note. "And how did you meet Scarlet?"

"He was assigned to me by the Department of Justice, I'm told. I mean, he just showed up in my interview room shortly after I was arrested."

"How soon after you were arrested?"

"I dunno. Maybe an hour? Maybe less. It was a long time ago now..."

"Yes. I can appreciate that." Rhodez sat for a long moment, contemplating what he'd heard. Then quietly he flipped out a tiny paper notepad and wrote his number on it.

"I'm assuming you have no holo..."

Houston showed the detective his naked wrist and nodded in the direction of the marshal at the front door.

"Ok. Look this is my contact IP. If you think of anything else, or anything else happens, be in touch, ok?" Rhodez folded the scrap of paper in two and dropped it onto the table in front of Houston.

Houston looked at it. "We don't have holos where I'm going."

"Yes, but you do have console access for good behavior," Rhodez told him. He stood up, placing a hand on the man's shoulder. "What you're going through is tough, but you'll get through it. Keep your head down and stay calm. I'll do what I can on this side. I don't believe you did it."

Houston's eyes started to tear up.

Rhodez gave the man's shoulder a comforting squeeze and then put one finger to his lips. The two men nodded and Rhodez made his way noisily out of the room. "Thanks for your time Mr. Houston," he raised his voice a few decibels as if to break the spell and return to a more distanced interaction for the sake of appearances to the babysitters.

As he left he noticed out of the corner of his eye Houston quietly picking up the note and discreetly pushing it into his pants pocket.

The marshal by the front door watched Rhodez approach down the hallway. He moved to open the door again. "Got what you needed?"

Rhodex nodded. "Yeah, not really. Open and shut," he shrugged. "Not all hunches pay off," he added feigning disappointment. He ambled out of the door. "Thanks for your help, marshal."

The marshal nodded and closed the door behind him.

Rhodez was smart enough not to rush back to his vehicle, across the sandy mud. Last thing he wanted was to tip off anyone who might be watching. He had something, and he knew precisely who he needed to look into next to blow the lid off this whole thing.

CHAPTER TEN

<u>Capitol Building, Spire, Estaria</u>

Commander Richard Ekks strode into his office. He had a matter of minutes before he had to turn right back around and head over to the other building for a meeting. Since he took this promotion his days had become meetings within meetings, packed alongside yet more meetings. Had he known beforehand what the day-to-day was going to be like he may have thought twice about accepting Ghetti's offer.

It was too late now. He was in.

And he was indebted.

He'd taken the bribe and one day he knew they'd come calling for more than just a seemingly inconsequential vote here, and a helping hand in a situation there.

He rummaged on his desk for the stim packets he'd brought in with him that morning. He remembered he'd swiped them into his drawer when his assistant came in. Though technically not outlawed they weren't exactly smiled upon in military culture.

He sat on his console chair and moved to open the drawer. His holo beeped. He checked it. A shudder rippled down his spine. It was a message from Ghetti, as if thinking about him prodded him to reach out.

He hit the decode protocol on the secret key that Ghetti had shared with him when they last met in person. The message decoded and displayed in Standard Estarian.

His eyes scanned the message quickly.

How we police the outer regions is a military decision, not a political one. We need you to make a statement in the media to this effect. Someone will reach out to you later today.

This was it.

This was the beginning of everything Raj Ghetti had talked to him about in their numerous clandestine meetings. Things were moving forward just as he said they would, and faster than Ekks had anticipated.

He typed a coded response to acknowledge the message and then deleted it. He sat staring into space for a few moments, contemplating the enormity of what he was a part of now. And then he remembered his meeting and stim packet.

He reached into his drawer quickly and located his stash, ripping open the packet and emptying the sachet of tart powder under his tongue. Then he discarded the packet, picked up his parade hat and hurried out of the door again.

Aboard *The Penitent Granddaughter*, Agresh Quadrant

Nickie stomped down the corridor with Grim hurrying along half a pace behind her, trying to keep up. "You know, you could just talk to them," he argued. "If they're Federation too then they'll probably tell you."

Nickie tapped the weapon in the holster of her right thigh. "I'll let Jean Dukes do the talking," she retorted.

Grim opened his mouth to protest again, but his words were lost to her. She was clearly fixated on the goal of finding out what their relationship was to her aunt.

Nickie. There is something else you need to know.

Oh, it's ok Meredith. I'm about to find out everything I need to know.

She swung around a corner of the corridor, her boots announcing her advance as only hard rubber on metal could. A cleaning bot felt the vibrations and scurried to the corridor wall just in time to avoid being kicked.

There is something you need to know before you go in there, guns waving. The ship's commander is a human, who has an AI in her head.

Nickie's pace slowed. Grim managed to catch up, panting now.

Bethany Anne?

No. Someone else.

There is no one else.

Well, it appears that is not quite true. Her artificial entity is relaying intel to me now. I think we can trust them not to harm us. It seems that we're each after the same thing.

A long life and lots of drugs?

No. Putting an end to illegal arms dealing in this sector.

You mean, they're the good guys?

Nickie and Grim arrived at the cargo hold door.

Yes. That's what my analysis is suggesting.

Shit. Just to be clear, I don't *get to royally kick Leath ass?*

'Fraid not.

Ok. So, what's our solution?

The entity contact is suggesting we reconvene at their base.

Yeah, like I'm that stupid.

I think you should reconsider. If there are any problems, I'll get us out of there. Plus, you have two of their people on board.

Fuck, I really have no choice. Nickie sighed. "Okay. Change of plan, Grim. We're not going to torture these folks for information."

Her fingers hovered over the door keypad, and she sighed again. "But we do need to get Durq out of there. Prolonged exposure to a stressful situation and who knows what state he'll be in."

"Okay," Grim said slowly. "And the humans?"

"Well, it appears we're on the same fucking side, so for now we're going to have to play nice."

Grim watched her carefully. "You're disappointed?"

"Well, you know me. I've been gearing up for action and all this is turning out to be more of a drama. Just need to ask them to put their goddamn guns away, else I'll have to teach them some manners on my ship."

Nickie, *The Empress* is trying to hail you. The female human's name is Molly. You're probably going to want to take this.

Nickie's hand dropped from the keypad. "Ok, patch her through."

"Hi there, Pretender," Nickie answered.

Molly's voice came back through her implant. "Hi there, Impostor."

Nickie pulled a face at Molly's retort but kept talking. "So, I'm about to head into the cargo hold. You wanna make sure your people know that we're friends and that we don't need to shoot each other?"

"Yes, one second."

Back on *The Empress* Molly hit mute and reopened the channel to Sean and Karina.

"Guys—Nickie is coming in. She's friendly. Well, not exactly in the social sense. But in terms of the op she's a friend. We've been going after the same targets. You're going to want to put your weapons down, please."

She heard a sigh on the line, and then the clicking of guns being disarmed and safeties going back on.

She muted them and unmuted the line to Nickie. "Okay, they're good."

"Good." Nickie stood back from the panel and then leaned against the wall, wanting to finish her conversation before she talked to the other humans on her ship. "So, I'm interested to know how you know about the Rangers."

"Oh, we're equally interested to know why you're *impersonating* a Ranger," Molly replied coolly. "But that can wait. Right now, we need to get away from this location in case that deal really is going down around here."

"Fine with me."

"May I suggest that we rendezvous at my base?"

"How do I know you're not laying a trap?"

"Did you miss the memo where Oz and Meredith figured out we're on the same side?"

"No. But still. I'd like some assurances."

Molly sighed, taking a moment to think. "Well, how about you keep my people on your ship and you can deliver them safely to my base when you're satisfied that we're not trapping you."

There was a frustratingly long pause on the line. Molly shot Joel a glance, showing her mild annoyance at this newcomer.

"That would be okay. I guess," Nickie responded eventually.

"Great. We're sending Meredith the coordinates now. See you back there. We'll put the kettle on."

The call disconnected, leaving Nickie wondering what the hell the woman had meant about a kettle.

She punched the access code into the keypad. A moment later the door slid slowly open to reveal Sean and Karina sitting on crates. Her gaze flicked around the room, looking for Durq. She found him, her supposed arms dealer, in the corner, hiding behind the pretend stack of guns.

Nickie raised her eyes to the ceiling. "Give me strength," she muttered exhaling sharply.

Aboard *The Empress*, Agresh Quadrant

Jack had been watching the whole interaction quietly from the back of the cockpit. Hearing the new plan, she relaxed. "I guess my services are no longer needed."

"Not at the moment," Molly confirmed.

Jack headed out of the cockpit and back to the lounge, allowing her heart rate to return to normal. Her military background had prepared her well for the game of hurry up and wait, and thankfully it also gave her to tools to unwind if it turned out the action was delayed or aborted.

Joel remained in the cockpit, smirking at the interaction with Nickie and watching Molly's reactions. Molly ignored him. "So, Oz? How exactly is this going to go when we get back?"

"You make tea. Play hostess. Show her around and let her see you're not monsters."

"Right and then what?"

"And then you and the prodigal granddaughter need to sit down and talk."

Molly exhaled sharply, sitting herself down in the nearest console chair. "Great. Just what I wanted. A mission turning into a babysitting task."

"She's not exactly a baby," Oz reminded her. "Besides, you still have to solve the problem of getting those weapons back."

"Well, she's young enough to have created this cluster fuck of a mission," Molly retorted. "It might be worth letting Sean and Karina know that if there is any funny business they have permission to... well, do whatever it is those Federation types do to get what they want."

Brock snorted again.

Joel's chest was bouncing up and down as he laughed silently, his arms folded across his chest.

Molly wasn't sure if it was because she had called them and their tactics Federation-types, or whether they were amused with her annoyance with Nickie. Either way, she was too distracted to care.

This girl was turning out to be a pain in her butt.

Aboard *The Penitent Granddaughter*, Agresh Quadrant

Sean and Karina stood motionless in the cargo hold. It was large and cold, and resembled something one might see on a docudrama about people trafficking.

This ship definitely has a dark history, Karina thought to herself.

"Okay," Oz told them through their audio implants. "Molly is talking with her right now. She's just outside the door." The pair exchanged looks as they listened to Oz's briefing.

"Molly is agreeing to leave you on the ship with them and for us to rendezvous the ships back at the base."

Sean spoke quietly through gritted teeth. "You mean we have to stay here with these crazy fuckers?"

"If it's any consolation," Oz explained, "Molly has given you permission to use any means necessary to stay alive. But I would warn against killing any of the crew members especially since they seem to have links with the Federation."

Sean huffed. "So what are we meant to do?"

"May I suggest making friends? You do know how that works, don't you Royale?"

Karina's eyes danced with humor, tickled by the interaction between her husband and the AI. "Hey, do you always manage to cultivate such hostility with everyone?" she asked Sean. "Or is it primarily AIs and EIs?"

Sean disarmed the ZF-1 he'd been holding. "Funny," he told her. "You didn't have to marry me!"

"Well, actually, I kinda did," she responded. "It was either that or rot in Dad's dungeon."

Sean started to answer her back but the door to the cargo hold beeped and slid open, revealing a smallish blonde human and a yellow Yollin.

Karina raised one hand in a hello. "Greetings be upon you," she said, smiling amicably.

Sean simply glared at the young female, pretending to be Ranger Two. He lifted his chin slightly, assessing her, yet saying nothing.

"I hear we're all going back to Gaitune," Karina attempted again.

"Yes. That's the plan," the human told them. "I'm Nickie. I will be your escort for today." She rested her hand on the holstered weapon on her right thigh. "Any funny business, and I'm sure you can guess what I'm capable of."

Sean's eyes narrowed as his gaze fell to the weapon strapped to her leg. "Jean Dukes."

Nickie looked a bit surprised but handled it well as she nodded. "You know your weapons."

Sean nodded. "Used to carry a set myself. Back in the day. You know… when the frontier was policed by the lone gunmen." He watched carefully to see if she picked up on the ranger reference, his brain searching for any clues as to who this girl might be. She didn't seem to recognize him, but she did react when he mentioned the lone gunmen.

Karina stepped forward, her hand outstretched. The Yollin took a step backward behind Nickie. "I'm Karina. This is Sean. Royale. We're both Royale."

Nickie stepped forward confidently and shook her hand. She narrowed her eyes at Karina. "You're not going to tell me you're brother and sister?"

Karina shook her head.

Nickie nodded in understanding. "Married," she concluded, with a slight smirk. "This is Grim," she told them. "He's the chef. Can make anything." She folded her arms, looking from one to the other expecting something but nothing was offered.

Grim stepped forward. "Except we're a little low on supplies right now," he added shaking Karina's hand now.

Karina smiled congenially. "That's okay. We've got plenty of food back at the base. We'll have you fed in no time, I'm sure."

Karina glanced back at Sean. He seemed a million miles away. "You okay honey?" she asked.

"Yeah. Fine. Just doing some calculations. How fast can this ship go?" he asked Nickie.

Nickie's expression went blank.

A voice came over the intercom to the cargo hold. "It was originally designed to travel at up to five hundred, but with a few enhancements we can push nearly six-fifty."

"Meaning we'll be back in Gaitune in..." Sean screwed up his eyes trying to do the calculation.

"A few hours," the voice responded. "I'm Meredith, by the way. I'm aware of you Sean Royale," she added mysteriously. Karina shot him another look, as if her earlier point about AIs and EIs was just being confirmed.

Sean's eyes widened. "Well, you have me at a disadvantage, Meredith, because I know nothing about you except that name. Want to explain?"

"Well," Meredith continued, "since we have a long ride ahead of us, and not much else in the way of entertainment, perhaps we can all have a nice talk?"

Sean ambled over to the crates. Durq panicked and scuttled away and hid behind Nickie. Sean pulled at some of the crates and arranged them like a seating area and plonked himself down on one.

It wasn't the most comfortable, but it would do.

"Sure thing, Meredith. Let's start from the beginning—as in, when you and Nickie left the Federation."

Nickie tapped a finger to her lips. "I don't think..."

He waved a hand. "It's okay," Sean reassured her, his tone gentler now. "I've been told to make friends rather than kill you. So, I suggest we get any secrets out of the way before we get back to base, because those folks out there understand a lot less about the goings on at the Federation than I do, and they might not be quite so understanding."

Nickie moved toward the crates and sat down, followed shortly by Grim, and then Karina.

Durq remained at what he perceived to be a safe distance. The making-friends phase of Sean's mission had begun.

CHAPTER ELEVEN

<u>Conference room, Special Task Force Offices, Undisclosed location, Estaria</u>

The Sark had already descended beyond the planet's horizon, leaving the last remnants of twilight bathing the streets in a reddish glow.

Rhodez strode purposefully from his car in the underground carport. He made his way into the secure facility. Passing through empty corridors, he accessed several security checkpoints, each demanding a little more confirmation that he truly belonged in the location. Eventually he emerged from the final elevator and headed into the office space.

His initial scan of the office showed him that no one was at their console. Instead, they were already assembled at the top meeting room. Realizing he must be late he strode quickly through the deserted office and took the steps up to the meeting room two at a time.

Now that he was closer he could see they were still talking amongst themselves. That meant they hadn't started yet. He made his way in, closing the door behind him and nodding deferentially to Mrs. Bates who was still sorting through an array of holo screens on her wrist holo.

Alisha caught his eye. "Here," she said, moving a chair out for him next to her. He hurried around to the other side of the table and sat down, noting that Joshua was watching. He guessed he wasn't happy that Alisha was giving him what might be deemed to be special treatment.

Thankfully Carol Bates seemed ready to start the meeting. A hush fell over the meeting room full of agents.

"Greetings," she announced. "It seems like today has been a productive use of time. Who wants to go first?"

No one moved, so Alisha raised her hand. "We can," she volunteered, drawing a playful glare from her partner in the process.

Carol gave her the nod and sat down.

Alisha tapped her holo and cued up some of her evidence to show on the meeting room's presentation holoscreen. "Our task was to investigate the former occupants of the positions filled last Thursday. Joshua and I took the undersecretary, one Robert Califray, to Garet Beaufort. Califray hadn't been reported missing, even to this day, but his apartment has been re-let, and his things sold off. His job was also given to someone else. When we went digging we found that no one had actually heard from him in person. It was only after his assistant went looking for him at his apartment that she received a message at the office explaining he wasn't coming back from vacation."

Joshua took over. "With the help of Cleavon, we were able to track down the origin of the message to a mocha shop in midtown. We checked it out. Cross-referencing the time of the message with payments made at the mocha shop we were able to narrow down potential senders to one known person of interest in this whole campaign."

He nodded to Alisha who tapped her holo to reveal the mocha shop image of Arnold Sloth.

There was a collective gasp in the room. All the agents here had been involved in discovering this man in the first instance over a year ago now.

"It's that the guy behind the smoke bomb at the university!" Soraya exclaimed.

"One and the same," Alisha confirmed. "Back then we discovered that he was a fixer for the Northern Clan, but the trail went cold. Plus, it was a few smoke bombs and kids." She added glancing over at Hans Duo on the other side of the table. "No offense," she added, suddenly remembering his involvement.

He waved his hand. "None taken."

Carol interjected. "So we think he sent the message impersonating the missing person. To what end?"

"To stop people from looking into Califray's disappearance," Alisha responded confidently.

"We're thinking he probably killed our guy," Joshua added grimly, "and then sent the message to stop anyone from looking into his disappearance."

Carol nodded, taking notes. "Right then," she drawled as she tapped her holo. "What's your next move?"

Alisha and Joshua exchanged looks. "We've put a watch out for Sloth. When he surfaces, we will want to interview him."

Carol tapped her lip. "People like that don't admit to anything. They lawyer up. When you find him, keep eyes on him and see what he leads you to. You'll end up with far more intel that way than if you bring him in and spook him."

"Yes, ma'am," they responded in unison.

Carol studied the pair for a moment. "And you might want to start digging carefully—and I *mean* carefully—into his replacement, too. Tread gently, because based on everything else we know, he's suspect for something."

Alisha took another note, as Carol shifted her attention. "Rhodez? You were on our embezzler. What did you turn up?"

Rhodez straightened up in his seat and took a breath. "I don't think he did it," he stated bluntly. "The sudden payments in close succession over a few days into an obviously traceable bank account. It wasn't him."

Carol regarded him skeptically for a moment. "And his confession?"

"Turns out he was strongly encouraged to take a deal for a smaller sentence after the police had started releasing the pressure on him. His attorney, Henry Scarlet, suggested it was the only way to get his sentence down from twenty years."

Elroy leaned forward. "Hang on, you can't get twenty years for embezzlement."

"Exactly," Rhodez agreed, pointing at his teammate, "and you'd think an attorney of the justice department would know that. But when I asked, it wasn't the police who had said anything about twenty years. That had come from Scarlet."

"So, we're thinking the attorney is dirty?" Carol clarified.

Rhodez nodded confidently. "Yes, ma'am. I was gonna run an analysis on his cases overnight, see if he has done anything like this before. Even now though, I think it's safe to assume he's in someone's pocket."

"Good work," Bates told him. "Elroy, Dhashana, Cleavon—where are we on protection details?"

Dhashana spoke for her team. "Suedermann and Carpe are both under constant surveillance. They have to continue with their work, but we have safe houses ready should the situation escalate. They're being watched around the clock by two agents each, and each potential target has been fully appraised of the situation. They know the risks, and we've recommended full protective custody which they've each declined. We've also got requests in with the security teams at each of the government buildings to increase security in their departments, too."

"Good." Carol's cold smile hardened. "If there is so much as a suspicious person or anything in chatter that suggests they're in danger, I want them pulled and put into protective custody. I

don't care what they say or how much they protest. It's out of
their hands at that point. Understand?"

"Yes, ma'am," Dhashana confirmed.

"Cleavon?" Carol said, turning back to the analyst.

Cleavon was prepared. "We've got the go-ahead for a bug on
Beaufort and his new undersecretary. We'll be planting it in the
offices tonight, posing as cleaning crew."

"When you say we, you mean?"

"Raza and myself," he confirmed. "Well, Raza mostly," he qual-
ified, shooting a look across to the athletic-looking Estarian. "I'll
be on point tapping their existing security feed so we can get in
and out undetected."

Carol nodded. "Ok good luck. Let me know as soon as you're
done with a holomessage."

"Yes, ma'am," he confirmed.

Carol checked a few more items with her team before
dismissing them. The meeting room emptied out with some
agents ready to complete their night-time missions, and the
others going home to get as much rest as they could before it all
started again the next day.

Hangar deck, Gaitune-67

The *Your Future's Devine* set down on the hangar deck, after
only a short delay due to security protocols. Nickie waited somewhat patiently as the others got their gear together and headed
out down the ramp into the new Federation-looking base.

I'm not comfortable with this, Nickie grumbled to Meredith in
her head.

She strode confidently down the ramp of her ill-acquired
ship. Her long, dirty blonde hair curled resentfully around her
face, defying all of the tonging and straightening she had put it
through the last time she showered.

Despite her attitude and unhealthy habits, she was athletic

and toned. As Molly watched her approach, she guessed it was probably on account of the nanocyte technology she must have been exposed to. She'd noticed changes in her own body after her pod doc experience, making it far easier to stay in good shape.

Grim had congenially invited the two humans to move ahead of him. He followed them down, his two set of boots padding gently against the metal grating. Durq hung back, but scuttled in between Grim up front, and Nickie reluctantly bringing up the rear. He looked like a fearful pet, caught between his two masters.

In light of recent revelations, it appears that this is going to be your closest contact with home in several years, Meredith reminded her.

That's exactly why I'm not happy about it. Plus, that Molly chick said AI.

Yes. I noticed that too.

How come she gets an AI and I only get an EI?

Meredith paused uncharacteristically. **Are you suggesting I'm not adequate?**

No. I'm just curious.

Maybe you can ask her. You know, when you sit down and talk.

I dunno. That's a bit... you know, personal, don't you think?

I wouldn't know. I'm a mere EI. I have no inkling of the social nuance of the situation.

Touché, Meredith.

The humans reached the hangar deck floor first, to be met by more of the crew. There were two human females she could see as she approached. One with pale white skin and one a chocolatey brown. Nickie's gaze flicked from one to the other trying to guess who she'd been talking to. It was strange seeing such a high density of humans in one place after all this time.

There were back slaps and hugs. A similar display of camaraderie that she had seen all the time with the troops back on the *Meredith Reynolds*. The very thought of it made her resent these people already.

Finally, she reached the bottom of the ramp, noticing that Durq kept his distance from the group but orientated himself closest to Grim. *Grim was such a people person,* she mused, idly.

The girl with the yellow hair and pale complexion moved toward her. "Greetings," she said. It was the same voice she had been dealing with. She looked less intimidating in person. "Welcome to Gaitune-67, home of the Sanguine Squadron."

The guy with her echoed the sentiment. "I'm Joel," he said, offering his hand. Nickie remembered the old human custom. And hated it. Nevertheless, she forced herself to be accommodating and shook both their hands.

"Nice to meet you. I'm Nickie. Nickie Grimes."

The human who had identified himself as Sean Royale reacted when she said her name but offered nothing.

"So you guys are Federation?" she asked, filing Sean's reaction away to follow up on later.

"Not exactly," Molly confessed.

Nickie glanced around at the ships all around. "But these are Federation ships. And Federation technology."

Molly smirked. "Is your EI telling you that?"

Nickie blushed. "Yes," she admitted, playing with her finger. "But I did grow up in the Federation."

She regretted the impulsive display of attitude immediately.

"Interesting," Molly remarked. She glanced sideways at Joel, noticing that he was studying the young lady for more clues. And probably a psychological profile.

Molly changed the subject. "I suppose we should let the General know you're safe."

Nickie felt her blood run cold. "No! Let's not. Please, don't do that."

Molly frowned. "Why not?"

"Because." She paused a moment. "Well, it's complicated."

"Are you on the run?"

"Not exactly."

"Well, what then? Are they looking for you?"

"No. At least… I doubt it. I'm… on leave."

Joel interjected. "With a Skaine ship?"

"Yeah," she snorted. "What about it?"

Molly pressed her lips together. "I think we need to have a talk before we go much further. And you need to fill us in on exactly what is going on, else I have a duty to report this to the Federation."

Not like you to toe the company line.

She's clearly not happy at the thought of me reporting this. I think I can use it.

That's admirably deplorable.

Watch and learn, Ozzy-baby.

"So, Nickie. What do you say? Wanna sit down and talk about this diplomatically?"

Nickie had folded her arms. She released one hand to wave it dismissively. "Whatever. *Fine.*"

Molly looked around at the accumulating personnel. "Okay, how about you and I head into the base conference room, and Joel, perhaps you could organize introductions and look after our guests?"

Joel straightened up, surveying the group that was mulling around. "Sure thing."

Molly clocked Paige heading down the stairs from the daemon corridor. "Perhaps you could get Paige to organize some beers and pizza for us in the conference room, whatever our guests would like. Maybe take them up to the safe house and make them comfortable?"

Joel smiled. "No problem."

Molly motioned to Nickie in the direction of the double doors off the side of the hangar deck. "After you," she said politely.

Nickie strode off toward the double doors, annoyed with herself as much as anything else.

Joel snapped his attention to the group that was assembled on the hangar deck.

"Okay," he announced, feeling like he had a bunch of new recruits. Karina and Sean flanked him as if they were his back up. "This is Karina and Sean." They waved their hands at the newbies. "I guess you guys have already met though," he added, a little embarrassed. He stepped forward and offered his hand to the Yollin.

"You are?"

"Grim. This is our friend Durq." Durq waved awkwardly and folded one arm across his body and held onto the opposite elbow.

Joel noticed the awkwardness and didn't push for the handshake.

Paige appeared during the introductions, the sound of her high heels on the hangar deck flooring heralding her arrival. "Hey, guys... how's i—"

The Skaine and the Yollin turned to greet her, and she jumped back in surprise. "Oh my!" she exclaimed more loudly than she had intended. She drew back and quickly clamped one hand over her mouth.

Sean chuckled. Karina immediately slapped him with the back of her hand, shutting him up.

"Paige," Joel explained, smirking himself, "these are our new friends. This is Durq and Grim," he indicated to one then the other.

Paige collected herself and caught her breath. "I'm so sorry. Greetings of the day upon you. I'm Paige," she said, stepping forward again to shake Grim's hand. When Durq didn't offer his she resorted to a shallow, awkward bow in his direction, unintentionally avoiding eye contact.

Maya joined them, and immediately had a similar reaction to the new species. Paige helped steady her by grabbing her arm, and making the introductions, albeit still somewhat nervously.

Joel intervened quickly. "Paige, would you like to take our guests upstairs and arrange some food and refreshments for them? Molly would like some beer and pizza in the conference room for her and our other guest, too, if you don't mind."

Paige peeled her eyes away from Grim and Durq. "Of course. No problem at all," she confirmed. She turned back to the newbies. "So, Durq and Grim." She smiled, making a concerted effort to learn and use their names. "Would you like to follow me? We'll get something fixed up for you."

"Thank you," Grim replied for the both of them. "That's very gracious of you."

Paige flashed another lopsided smile and then ushered the two across the hangar deck and out of the base. Maya wandered alongside them, curious to know more about their visitors. She'd never seen a Yollin or Skaine in the flesh.

Neither had many of the others.

Brock and Crash had been watching from a short distance, casually obscured by *The Empress*. As the visitor party disappeared across the hangar deck, they collected in a group with Sean and Karina.

"Well, this is certainly a turn out for the books!" Brock commented excitedly.

"You're telling me," Sean agreed. "Back in my day we'd be ass-whooping Skaines left, right, and center.

Karina glared at him.

"Oh, they'd be returning fire," he protested. "They were badasses. The group of them." He paused, watching the party ascend the stairs to head back to the safe house. "That Skaine doesn't look right in the head though. They're normally more…"

"Aggressive?" Joel offered.

"Annoyingly so," Sean finished, his head cocked in curiosity.

"Looked like a scared pussycat to me," Karina commented. At that exact moment Neechie showed up, appearing a yard in front of them. He walked a few paces to where the strangers had been standing and then disappeared again.

Karina and Joel glanced at each other, eyes wide in both amazement, and amusement.

Brock scratched his head and rejigged the pack on his back. "Okay, well, we've got shit to do," he announced, changing the subject. "No doubt we'll have to try this mission again in a few hours. I for one want to have eaten, rested and have the ship ready when we do"

Crash mumbled something in agreement and the group broke away in pairs going about their business.

CHAPTER TWELVE

<u>Meeting room, Special Task Force Offices, Undisclosed location, Estaria</u>

"So, what did we find?"

Carol Bates was on the case this morning. Her crisp white blouse was tucked elegantly into the atmosuit pants she wore. She was ready for either a mission or a meeting and judging by the hands on her hips the team suspected she was shooting for both right now.

Alisha raised her hand, drawing the go-ahead to report in.

"We've got eyes on Sloth. Agents are following him at a safe distance. As soon as we can pinpoint his routine we'll be bugging his living and workspace. We still like him for the disappearance of Califray and we're looking for further evidence of his involvement."

Rhodez raised his hand and waited for the nod from Carol. "I've been thinking about this. He could easily have given instructions to Scarlet to sway his plea. Can we keep a patch running in the data to look for any links between Sloth and Scarlet?"

Alisha made a note. "Sure. Just get us all the known addresses and facial images and we'll add them into the analysis."

Carol sat down, clearly mulling the situation. "Rhodez, are the money trails telling you anything?"

Rhodez shook his head. "We're not sure yet. We're letting the system do the heavy lifting to figure that out. It's offline at the moment but the minute it comes back on our request is in the queue. The overnight sequence we ran on our local servers though showed that in terms of his cases, he had a good closure rate... but a much higher percentage of his cases are closed by them pleading down higher charges."

Carol pressed her lips together. "Which would suggest that this is a strategy our attorney uses to close a case."

Rhodez tilted his head thoughtfully. "Yeah, the only problem is that his defendants end up getting charged, even if they didn't do anything."

There were the usual check-ins about the surveillance operations and some mundane updates about details that were coming to light as they watch the two innocent government workers and the shady Arnold Sloth. It didn't take long for Carol to wrap up what they needed to talk about and what could be put into a download for their daytime reading. Then she dismissed everyone. "Thanks, people," she told them. "Good work so far."

She sat down at the table again, clearly not in a rush to go anywhere. Hans Duo hovered, interpreting it as a sign that they needed to continue their conversation.

Hans waited for everyone to leave before getting the door.

"So, you heard all that about Charlie team thinking that Sloth is involved in the disappearance of their Califray?"

"Yes, ma'am. But you're not buying it."

"No. I'm not. This is classic Sneaky Steve." Vindication arose in Carol's steely eyes.

"What would you like me to do?"

"Well, we have agents on Sloth, so there is nothing for you to do right now. But at some point, Sloth is going to slip up and give us a lead. I'm hoping that it's one that's going to let us locate Sneaky Steve… And then you'll be back in play."

Hans nodded and got up. He didn't need any more explanation. He knew what his role was. "We'll bide our time then," he concluded. Carol nodded, and he headed out of the door.

Base conference room, Gaitune-67

Molly paced in front of the table. There was a heavy atmosphere of seething resentment hanging over the conference room. Molly tried her best to ignore it, but there was something within Nickie that reminded her of herself not so long ago. She felt bad for her, but there was still an urgent mission that needed fixing. And fast.

"So what were you doing out there?" she asked simply.

Nickie sat at the table looking straight ahead, avoiding eye contact with Molly. "Same thing you were no doubt."

"Which was?"

The young woman met Molly's eyes with a flash of fire in her own. "Trying to stop those scumbags from doing a deal. Maybe even taking them out of the game. One less ship of mercenaries out there terrorizing the frontier."

Molly halted at the other end of the room. She closed her eyes for a moment, trying to understand where all the hatred and anger was coming from.

She attempted a clarification. "You don't like Leath?"

"Not particularly, but I really have an annoyance for the Skaines," Nickie shrugged. "Evil creatures. Only out for themselves, completely happy with enslaving any race they come across."

Molly pulled out one of the antigrav chairs and sat down. "I can agree with the sentiment that they need to be stopped. But tell me, what *was* your plan?"

Nickie had been free-flowing sanctimony but suddenly

stopped. She regarded Molly carefully. "Why do you need to know?"

"So we can figure out our next steps. Both those ships are still out there, and they have the weapons. The very weapons I've been charged to take out of circulation."

"On orders from Reynolds?"

Molly paused before answering. "Yeah, that's right. Which brings us back to how you know so much about the Federation."

Nickie rolled her eyes. "I just do, all right? As for our game plan, we need to find a way to track those fucktards. I need to get back on my ship to look at some data."

Molly put her hand up in a stopping motion. "Okay. In a minute. Just right now, tell me what your plan was. You were going to meet with the Leath and pretend to be making the exchange. Then what?"

"Well, obviously I don't have the weapons, but once I knew for certain they were after them then I could pass judgment and take their asses out."

Molly reacted internally to the idea of someone passing judgment but tried to put it aside. She regarded the slightly built adolescent, who clearly wasn't that much younger than her. "The three of you?"

"No, those two are pretty useless when it comes to dishing out ass-kickings, even if Grim has more heart to help than ability. So just me."

Molly didn't take her eyes from Nickie. It was as if she were waiting for Nickie to reveal something else to her. Something that would explain how one human female thought she could go up against a ship full of Leath.

She's enhanced.

How do you know?

I'm talking with her on board EI.

Molly leaned closer, as if trying to see the EI peering out from behind Nickie's eyes. Nickie shifted uncomfortably and started pacing to avoid the scrutiny.

Fascinating.

Yeah. Seems it's pretty normal for that core group of friends and family.

So it's not a Federation thing?

More of a Bethany Anne thing, by the sounds of it. Something like a reward for those who took a chance on her to save her old world, against all odds.

Hmm.

Nickie had moved on from the past moments and responded with outright anger. "If you hadn't shown up I'd have handled the Leath and been on my way to rain carnage down on the Skaines by now." Her eyes darted around the room, giving her the look of a caged animal.

Molly shook her head definitely. "Nope. Sorry. I can't let you go after the Leath now. They're wanted by their government, so I can't risk their authorities getting hold of them. Federation orders. Got to play nice when inter-civilization relations are involved."

"Well, if you hadn't been interfering in the first place."

Molly put her hand up. "Acting on behalf of the Federation is hardly interfering."

"I disagree. You don't think that the Federation is all about interfering in other peoples' business?"

"Fighting your own personal vendettas and going vigilante on the sector isn't interfering?" Molly shot back.

"You don't know what you're talking about. You're just all high and mighty with a stick up your ass because Uncle Lance left you in charge of a fucking asteroid base in the middle of nowhe—"

"Young lady!"

Molly froze, immediately wishing she could take back her last words.

Shit. I just became my mother.

Young adults will do that to you.

But I'm barely older than that myself.

Somehow, I think you've grown up without realizing it. You've become your Mom.

Oh, fuck me. Don't say that.

Molly could feel Oz chuckling away in the back of her cortex. It tingled. She tried scratching her head.

Knock it off, Oz. This is serious.

Nickie had stopped ranting.

Well, seems to have had some effect at least.

Maybe there's hope for your parenting skills after all.

Please don't jinx me.

"Okay," Molly began again, more composed now. "As I see it, you want to take both parties out, and I need to get those weapons back."

Nickie seemed to be making an effort to cooperate. "Yeah," she said slowly. "How about I go after the Skaines then? My preference is kicking Skaine ass anyway…"

"Fine," Molly agreed. "And we'll go after the Leath ship. We just need to figure out where our respective targets have gone."

Kitchen, Safehouse, Gaitune-67

Paige moved ahead of her new group of guests, leading the way through the safe house into the kitchen. "Do you guys like pizza?" she asked over her shoulder. "I've got the best place in the system on speed dial. It's one of two pizza joints on this forsaken rock, but it even does a mean meat-free veggie stuffed crust."

"Actually," Grim cut in as he followed her into the kitchen. "If you have the supplies, then I could probably rustle us up something."

She frowned, thinking. "I don't know what we've got. But

you're our guest. We should be looking after you, not having you slave away cooking for us."

"Oh *please*," he chuffed. "It's no bother. In fact," he confided conspiratorially, "I find it rather relaxing. It would be nice to take my mind off the life on a ship and all the intrigue for a while."

Paige strode over to the larder as the others filed into the kitchen, she opened the door. "We have a ton of stuff in here." She pointed to one of the big silver fridges at the other end of the kitchen. "The cold stuff is in there."

Grim inspected the oven, tracing his fingers over the dials and knobs on the top surface. "Looks good," he said, satisfied. He turned to Maya and Durq. "Is everyone good with pizza?"

There was a resounding 'yes' from the group, including Maya whose enthusiasm had just picked up.

Durq nodded excitedly. "Oh yes indeed."

Grim rubbed his hands together and clapped a couple of times. "Great. I'm going to need a mixing bowl or two. Paige, perhaps you can find me some utensils. Maya, I'll need flour and butter first of all, and see if you get the cheese out so it can start acclimating to room temperature. Actually, I feel like making an iron-rich soup as an appetizer, so any vegetation you have, let's get that out too..."

The kitchen suddenly became a hive of activity as the two girls played sous-chef to Grim's instructions. It wasn't long before mouth-watering aromas filled the common room.

Paige washed the remaining dough from her hands. "Hey, I should go and catch up with the rest of the team," she announced. "You guys gonna be okay in here for a bit?"

Grim nodded, stirring his soup. "We're great here," he confirmed, beaming.

"Excellent!" Paige took her apron off, throwing it over the back of a chair as she left.

Maya had been sitting at the kitchen table, chopping vegetables. She scraped her chair back. "I guess with an impending mission, margaritas are out of the question, but how about some virgin ones?"

Paige chuckled to herself as she heard Maya taking over the role of hostess, seamlessly.

Base workshop, Gaitune-67

Paige clip-clopped down the last few stairs into the workshop. "Ah, here you all are!" she announced.

Sean and Karina were working on some weapons. Sean appeared to be cleaning one and reassembling it. Karina was loading something that Paige didn't even recognize.

Brock had his back to everyone, working away at one of the consoles and Crash seemed to be studying some maps of the sector they had been in. "I guess this is the most likely station," he said to Brock. Brock acknowledged it, but it didn't look like any surprising revelations were happening.

Paige stood with one hand on her hip and looked at the crew. "So? Is anyone going to explain to me what's going on? Who are our new guests?"

Karina smiled. "Thought you got the introductions?"

Paige returned a sardonic half-smile. "I did. But I still don't know what happened or what they're doing here."

Brock wheeled around. "We're still trying to figure out what happened, and who these folks really are." He grabbed a seat and offered one to Paige at the same workbench. "Here's what we know so far. We went in to intercept the Skaine ship before the exchange. But so did they, posing as Skaines and trying to intercept the Leath, pretending to have the weapons."

Paige tipped her head forward. "You're kidding?"

Brock shook his head grimly. "Not even slightly. Couldn't make this shit up… Anyway, turns out the girl, their leader, has some kind of EI bot in her head. Bit like Molly, but not. Apparently put there by the Federation."

Paige put a hand to her chest to steady herself. "You're kidding? Why?"

Brock shrugged. "Not entirely sure but reading between the lines of what Oz is picking up from their discussion she is some kind of Etheric Empire baby."

"A *what* now?"

"I dunno. Something to do with the Empress's nearest and dearest getting special treatment. They get certain enhancements and tech implanted to keep them safe and allow them certain advantages. In exchange for helping her, she looked after their children who could become a target by providing them a bonus. We aren't too sure if those are the right details, but it's probably close I'm thinking."

Paige was speechless. Her mouth hung slightly open as she parsed the information.

"Anyway," Brock continued, "the details are vague, but essentially we're kind of on the same side."

Joel wandered back into the workshop from the hangar deck, followed by Pieter. They both looked weary. Joel's uniform had oil on it. He loitered, listening to the conversation, and Pieter took the kit he was carrying and shoved it back into one of the cabinets.

"All ok?" Brock checked with Pieter.

"Yeah. We just got done recalibrating the shield appearance. I've diverted full power back to the protection frequencies. No more pretending to be Leath."

Joel sat down on a stool on the opposite side of the bench to Paige. "Yeah. Let's hope we don't need to disguise ourselves again. That was a bitch to reset."

Brock turned to him. "Well, if it's any consolation, while you guys were doing that we've managed to recheck all the cloaking systems."

"And?" Joel asked.

"Well, it's all working fine. So we definitely weren't seen by the real targets and it was just a stroke of bad luck that we managed to bump into Nickie and Co."

Joel scratched his head. "Still doesn't explain why the other ships didn't show up. They can't have been in and out in the time we were cloaked and unable to see them."

Brock sighed. "We can only guess at this point. Either they saw us heading in, or something changed. Somehow they managed to communicate with each other and change their rendezvous point, either as a result of catching onto us, or just through paranoia. Meredith checked their job system, and nothing changed on there. No alerts or anything... so I'm assuming the latter."

Joel bobbed his head. "Okay. Does Molly know?"

Brock shook his head. "She's still busy with Princess Federation." He chuckled at his own joke. "But Oz will be letting her know as soon as she gets a moment."

Joel sighed, heaving himself off the stool. "Okay great. I'm gonna shower and get some rack time. Sounds like we've only got a few hours at most before we need to head back out again."

Brock got up too. "Good plan. Don't forget to leave your boots by the door. When we get the go we're going to have to literally jump."

"Yeah," Joel muttered, dragging himself across to the stairs. "Let's hope I get at least forty winks."

Paige watched him go. "Hang in there," she encouraged. "It'll be over soon, and then we'll be back to routine."

Sean and Karina had been talking among themselves. "Don't say that!" he called over. "We'll never catch a moment's peace."

Karina grinned. "I never had you pegged as superstitious!"

Sean chuckled, clicking the final piece of his weapon together. "New habit," he confessed. "Since things just seem to be jinxed."

"Okay," Paige declared. "I need to get back up there. Pizza should be ready soon if you're hungry. Grim is cooking and so far, it's smelling a-ma-zing!"

ELL LEIGH CLARKE & MICHAEL ANDERLE

There were excited grunts and exclamations about the home-made pizza as Paige made her way back to the stairs and followed Joel back up to the safe house.

Base conference room, Gaitune-67

Looks like we've got a lead. On the Skaine ship, anyway.

Tell us, both, Molly instructed him.

Oz's voice came over the conference room audio. Molly noticed that Nickie wasn't at all taken aback by it. Nor did she seem particularly impressed.

"There have been reports of a Skaine shooting at a nearby trading post. Sources are saying it looks like a bar brawl that got out of hand."

Molly shook her head. "That's original."

Nickie agreed. "Skaines," she hissed through gritted teeth. "And how many innocent bystanders have been killed just because they drank too much?"

"I don't have a report on that yet. This is still just chatter. Station police are arriving on the scene right now."

"Looks like we have a beat on where the Skaines might be," she determined. "But no way of knowing whether the Leath have taken possession of the weapons yet... or if the Skaines still have them."

"How are we so sure it's our Skaines?" Nickie asked.

"It's the nearest trading post to where the exchange went down."

Nickie interjected. "And if the Skaines are in a bar it's probably because they've got their score, which means they've already exchanged their weapons for money."

"Shit. Well, that's your target identified." Molly cursed, hands back in her hair. "Now we just need to find the Leath."

"Well," Nickie got up from the table and started toward the

132

door. "Looks like I've got my work laid out for me. I'll just grab my crew and get going."

She stopped in her tracks. "But I am curious… about how you know my aunt."

Molly narrowed her eyes, an idea striking her. "Well, I guess if we were *friends*, we'd be able to sit around and talk about it. But it sounds like we both have work to do…"

Nickie hesitated. "Well… hang on. What about if I help you get a jump on the Leath? After all, it wouldn't hurt to look like you had some Skaine muscle behind you, and honestly? You're more likely to get close with a Skaine ship than a Federation one."

Molly thought for a moment. "Well, that would be pretty cool."

"Great."

"But what about the Skaines?" she asked.

Nickie waved her hand. "No biggie. I'll catch up with them eventually. And besides, if they're at the bar, they'll be a while sleeping it off and then getting drunk all over again. That kind of cash from the weapons they were selling will keep them going a while."

Molly frowned, just realizing something. "So what, you're some kind of Skaine hunter?"

Nickie scoffed. "Not really." She paused, her eyes looking up and to one side. "Well… actually, yeah. Maybe I am. Though I prefer to think of myself as more a lone ranger."

"With friends."

Nickie chuckled quietly. "Every ranger needs a crew. Gets tedious otherwise."

"Which brings us back to the question of why you're impersonating a Ranger…"

Nickie looked awkward. "Well, it's complicated."

"Try me." Molly watched her adamantly.

"It's not entirely an untruth," Nickie started to explain slowly.

"I was trained by my aunt. She *was* Ranger Two. And she gave me her badge when she left… so… I just picked up where she left off. That's all."

Molly studied her. "So you're admitting you're part of the Federation after all?"

"Empire, but yeah. My grandfather was in with the Empress herself. One of the Bitches. The personal guard."

Molly sat back down, glad to have Nickie finally confirming what Meredith had already told them. "And you're… enhanced?"

"Yeah."

"With a computer in your cortex and everything?"

Nickie nodded, and then frowned, leaning forward a touch to look at Molly more closely – as if peering into a mirror. "How did you get yours?" she asked. "Are we related?"

Molly shook her head and smirked. "No… mine happened in a completely unexpected, non-Federation kind of way."

Nickie waved her hands indicating at everything around them. "So how come you have all this?"

Molly leaned back and threw her hands in the air. "Sometimes I ask myself that question too. I guess there was a position going and I just fit the bill. Right time, right place."

Nickie narrowed her eyes. "I'm not sure I believe that. And I'm not sure you truly believe that either. Knowing Uncle Lance…"

"*Uncle* Lance?"

"Yeah. But not by blood, obviously. But, you know. The kids of the Bitches all grew up around this Empire-or-call-it-Federation-if-you-want shit and so we're all treated like the nieces and nephews of the others. You know."

"Yeah…" Molly said slowly. "There's only one other person I know who calls Lance *Uncle* though."

Nickie sat up. "Oh yeah? Who would that be?"

Molly shook her head. "We'll get to that. Maybe. Right now, bigger fish to fry."

"Like tracking down those Leath?" Nickie said.

Molly nodded. "Exactly. And I think I have an idea. But you're probably not going to want to be here for the next few minutes."

"Why? What are you thinking?"

"I've got a plan, but you're going to owe me *big-time*, because this is going to wreck my otherwise perfect record of always getting my guy."

"What are you going to do?"

"Why don't you head back to your ship and pull off the exact ship registration number for the Leath we're after, and ping it back to me on my holo?"

"Ok," Nickie agreed, suspicious again.

"Then head up to the safe house, I'll meet you there."

Nickie nodded abruptly and then strode out of the conference room.

You'll help Meredith find her way around?

Yeah. She's already tapped into the wireless. I've allowed her access to basic layout and schematics. Nothing more.

Good. Thanks, Oz. Now let's see if we can get a quick meeting with the General.

Aye, aye, Captain!

CHAPTER THIRTEEN

Base conference room, Gaitune-67

The three-dimensional holoscreen opened out from the center of the conference table and unfolded to display an image of Lance's office.

Molly waited, peering curiously at the empty office. She heard a scuffling off camera, then a thud, like a box of books hitting the floor.

Lance appeared through the open door from his main office.

"Ah, Molly. Hello." He sat down at his console chair and settled in. "To what do I owe the pleasure?"

Molly braced herself internally. "I need some help, sir."

Something flickered across his face. *Was it a smirk?* "Help with what?" he asked innocently.

"With tracking down a particular Leath ship," she admitted.

He raised his chin, contemplating. "I take it the exchange went ahead, then?"

"Yes, sir. We ran into some... hiccups."

"Hiccups?"

"Yes, sir."

"And what form did these hiccups take?" he asked, looking more and more interested by the moment.

Molly racked her brains and spoke fast. "It was a delicate operation. The slightest timing discrepancy would have had it fail. However," she continued quickly, "we still have the element of surprise. Neither party knew that we were there, or that we're onto them."

Lance regarded her carefully. "Well, by the sounds of it, if you're asking for the Leath location, you're not onto them."

Molly's gaze hit the desk in front of her. "Yes, sir."

Lance steepled his hands and sat forward. "Well. I suppose I could call in a favor and get you the coordinates. All on the down-low, of course. If anyone were to ask where you got them, it can't be from me."

"Of course, sir. So, you have a way of getting them?"

"I have a guy who can pull their tracking data. Send me the ship's registration. It may take a few hours, but you need to be ready to move. Once we have them there is no guarantee they'll stay at that location for long. Especially not if they're carrying a payload."

"Yes, sir. Of course, sir. And thank you."

Lance leaned forward to terminate the call. He paused as if having another thought. "And Molly?"

"Yes, sir?"

"Let's not screw up again."

"Yes, sir."

The screen went blank and folded itself away. Molly exhaled slowly.

Looks like we got away with that one.

Barely.

You think he suspects anything?

Like 'the penitent granddaughter' being in our mix?

Yeah.

I wouldn't like to speculate. There is one thing ADAM is

really good at though, and that is knowing everything *all* the time.

That's true. You think he might be testing us to see if we come clean?

Maybe.

Is there anything in any of those rules and regs that say we have to report on any contact with Federation personnel, on leave or otherwise?

Nope. Already checked. Nada.

Molly slumped back in the chair for a moment, her hands on her head and fingers interlocked. *Well... I guess that's decided then.*

She heaved herself up wearily. *Lemme know the second we get those coordinates and put the crew on standby for a quick turnaround.*

Aye, Captain.

Molly smiled to herself. *I'm going to join the others for food.*

Kitchen, Safehouse, Gaitune-67

Grim, Durq, Nickie, Paige and Maya sat around in the kitchen eating. It appeared that cooking together was an excellent bonding exercise.

"So *then* what happened?" Paige and Maya watched transfixed as Grim continued the story.

"Well, I'm not sure. I was still slipping around in the kitchen, trying to get my shit together. Meanwhile, her highness," he gestured at Nickie who was slurping on a smoothie, "managed to get all the way to the control room, past goodness knows how many Skaines."

Nickie tried to suppress a grin, with the straw in her mouth.

Grim soaked up the captive audience. "The next thing I heard was a bunch of explosions and weapons going off. By the time I got to the bridge she was already declaring to the space-station's commander that she needed refueling!"

Maya and Paige laughed hysterically. Even Nickie was amused and enjoying the moment.

Molly arrived just as Grim finished his story. "Sounds like it's all fun and games up here!" she remarked.

Grim jumped to his feet. "Please sit, Molly." He set a bowl in front of her and then ran back to the cooker where he had a pot on the boil. "I'll have some more pizza ready in a moment, but in the meantime, try this." He scooped a liquid into the bowl. It was a relatively natural and healthy-looking color.

"What is it?" she asked sniffing at it skeptically.

"Grim's not a warrior," Nickie explained, "but he is a damn good cook. Just try it."

Molly picked up a spoon from the center of the table and tasted it. Flavors exploded on her tongue and the soup trickled down the inside of her throat almost as if it was already nourishing her. "Wow! That is amazing!"

"See," Nickie said, victoriously.

"I do!" Molly agreed, taking another spoonful.

Grim blushed. "Just something I rustled up from a few things you had in the stores already."

Paige interjected. "I was going to order pizza like you said, but—"

"I insisted," he continued. "Least I could do after all your hospitality – and, you know, not shooting us on sight," he added only half-jokingly.

Nickie breathed out through her nose, marginally entertained now.

"So," Molly said between spoonfuls. "It looks like we might have a way to extract the current location of the Leath vessel. As soon as we receive it we'll need to go."

Nickie pulled her mouth down at the corners. "Impressive. How did you manage that?"

"Oh, you know. Friends in high places," she responded, winking.

Nickie nodded, wary of steering clear of any conversation

which might prompt more questions about her history with the Federation. "Friends in the Federation?" she ventured.

Molly smiled. "I cannot confirm nor deny that statement, but let's just say, it was better that you *weren't* in the room."

Nickie's face softened for the first time since she'd arrived on Gaitune. "Thanks," she said gently.

"Any time."

"So," Paige continued pulling Molly's attention to the next topic. "It looks like we've had some progress on the ground with the Academy."

"Oh?"

She grinned and then shot a look in the direction of their uncleared guests. "Details will have to wait until later, but it appears our impending doom has evaporated away."

Molly's next spoonful slopped back in her bowl, her hand and mouth coordination forgotten. "What happened?"

"Ben'or," Paige responded simply. "And your Mom." She smiled again. "Details later. But I figured you should know so you can chillax."

Molly returned her attention to her soup and mopped up a splash with her napkin. "Yeah. Wow. That's a huge relief." Just hearing the news, the others seemed to relax too. It was like a weight had been lifted from all of them, freeing them up to focus on the newcomers and their impending mission.

Grim sniffed the air, getting up to shuffle back around to the oven. "I think that this second pizza is just about ready." He donned the oven gloves and retrieved the molten cheesy delicacy, carefully placing it on the countertop.

"Nom nom," Durq muttered as the smell wafted through the kitchen. Molly noticed that even he looked more relaxed now, albeit probably on account of the lack of guns being waved in his face.

"Okay, who wants the first piece?" Grim asked. There was a clattering of chairs and plates as everyone got up to receive their next slice of heaven. Grim chuckled, thrilled that his culinary skills were being so appreciated for a change. "Next one has to go down to our friends' downstairs," he warned them.

Safehouse, Gaitune-67

"Okay, folks," Oz announced over the safe house and base intercom. "We've got the coordinates. Time to move out."

Joel was in his quarters, lying on his bed, eyes closed. He opened one eye, then shut it again. He was exhausted. That last mission had taken it out of him for some reason, and the prospect of such a fast turnaround sucked.

He took a deep breath, willing himself to push the tiredness aside. Counting to three in his mind, he opened both eyes and swung his legs off the bed.

"No rest for the wicked," he mumbled to himself, grabbing his boots and slipping them on as he had hundreds of times before. A minute later he was heading down the corridor, zipping up his atmojacket.

"Pizza?" Grim asked, offering him a box from a stack of boxes he had ready in the common room.

Joel took the box. "You packed some up for us?"

"All part of the service," Grim replied with a slight bow.

Joel couldn't believe his luck. He took a sniff of the amazing food smell coming from the package and realized just how hungry he was now. "Wow. That's really decent of you. Thanks, Grim!"

"Of course. And good luck out there. Whatever the plan is. I'll be staying out of harm's way. I'm a cooker, not a fighter!"

Joel chuckled. "I guess staying safe is a good plan, then. Thanks, Grim. I hope we get to spend more time together at some point when this is all over."

"As do I, Mister Joel."

Joel patted the Yollin on the shoulder and then strode down the hall to the workshop door.

Meanwhile, everyone else seemed to be collecting their special packages of home-made pizza and heading in the same direction.

Joel followed the crowd through the safe house, down the basement stairs, through the workshop and back out into the main base. When he arrived onboard the ship, Molly was already there doing up her belt in the lounge. The ship was already humming, ready to lift off as soon as the doors were closed. Joel made his way straight to Molly and sat down next to her.

"Bringing lunch with you?" she asked, nodding at the box.

"I didn't get the chance to eat."

"You feeling okay?"

"Yeah. Just a little tired, that's all. So did you find out much more about our guest?"

Molly shook her head. "Not anything useful at this point. She seems to have a chip on her shoulder about her grandfather, more than the Federation itself, but I think over the years it's just become generalized."

"I'm going to excuse the pun."

Molly sniggered, realizing what she had said.

Joel strapped himself in and started opening the pizza box. "Do we have a plan for when we get to these coordinates yet?"

Molly shook her head. "Not beyond the obvious. We'll know more as we approach. Coordinates look like they're for some kind of shipping port – which would make sense. If they've just scored their weapons then they're probably looking to exchange some of them for parts and supplies, I guess."

She shrugged. "But like I said, we'll know more soon."

"And then I can put together an operationally realistic plan in the five seconds we have between seeing the target and engaging."

"Exactly," she agreed, patting his arm.

Joel snorted, and tipped his head back against the headrest for a moment.

She nodded at his pizza. "You should eat now, though. Won't take us long to get there."

He glanced down at it. "Smells amazing."

"It really is," she agreed.

"Ladies and gentlefolk," Crash's voice announced over the intercom. "We're about to leave the base for Take Two of this mission. If you could take your seats and engage your seat belts, Empress Spacelines will be ascending any minute now. If you look out of the port side window you will see our local example of a Skaine ship. Take note and commit this to memory, because it's unlikely you'll see such a specimen in these parts any time soon."

Crash continued in his normal pilot-announcer voice. "If you'd like to take holoimages, please consider your feed followers when choosing to post publicly. And please remember, any unauthorized footage will be removed by our in-house AI. Consider yourself warned."

The Empress gently lifted off, and although Crash was only joking with his crewmates in his announcement, more than a few of them shuffled over to the port side windows in the lounge to get a look at the Skaine ship that was taking off just ahead of them.

"The power of suggestion," Molly mused, remembering how she'd use that many a time to manipulate co-workers for amusement in her pre-Sanguine Squadron days.

Aboard *The Empress*, Skipum Wharf, Agresh Quadrant

Crash brought *The Empress* to a pause fifty kilometers out from the shipping port. "Yep, definitely them," he said, punching in on the registration plate on the hull on the holofeed on the main display.

Molly studied the holoscreen. "Great. If they're here they're either in for repairs or restocking on parts. Let's get Nickie on the line."

Crash punched a few keys and Nickie connected with them on a second holo screen and over the cockpit audio.

"You seeing what I'm seeing?" Nickie chimed confidently, bypassing normal pleasantries. Molly noticed she had her feet up on her console unit in the bridge.

"That this is our target?" Molly confirmed.

"Exactly."

Molly glanced over at Joel to check he was watching before she continued the conversation. "So any ideas for retrieving the weapons and immobilizing the troops?"

Nickie looked like she was actually thinking. "Dunno," she said reluctantly. "Just blowing up the ship with a torpedo seems a bit overkill – given that the good people of this port probably didn't do anything I'd object to."

Joel watched Molly's expression as she stood, hands on hips facing the main screen. "You think?" she scoffed.

The sarcasm seemed lost on Nickie. "Yeah. I'm thinking we should dock and then go in and take out a few of them manually."

Molly was about to protest when Nickie kept talking. "We don't need to kill them all. Just a few – just to show that we mean business."

Molly's frown deepened. "How about we set the weapons to stun and just immobilize them and tie them up? I need to call in the Leath authorities, but more importantly, we need to get those weapons off that ship before they get there."

Nickie paused for a moment. "Okay," she agreed reluctantly. "We can do it the un-fun way. My preliminary scan is showing there are about two hundred crew, fifty-something of whom are gathered in the ship. Might be a bar or mess hall, or something."

Joel stood up and edged closer to Molly to talk in a low voice.

"From the schematics, it looks like we could probably confine them to that area and take control of the ship separately."

Oz's voice came over the intercom. "Meredith has suggested taking control of the ship's secondary controls and putting it in lockdown. Apparently, she's done this before to great effect."

"Okay, we'll do that," Molly agreed. "But only on my signal, when we're ready to storm the station. We need to be in position first."

"Crash, take us in," she instructed, touching his shoulder briefly. "Nickie, perhaps you could dock on the port side. We'll take the starboard. That will give us two angles of approach once we get boots on the station."

Nickie nodded, taking her feet off the console and standing up. "No problema," she agreed. "We'll get ready. See you on the flip side. *Penitent Granddaughter*, out."

Molly shook her head, trying to maintain her patience. "Hey... Nickie, wait!" she called. "Make sure you wait for my signal. We all strike together, got it?"

"Yeah, yeah, I've got it. Stick up ass, et cetera, and so on." She ended the call connection with an exaggerated roll of her eyes.

"That girl!" Molly growled in frustration.

She turned to see Pieter and Joel sniggering quietly. "Stick up ass!" Joel chuckled. "Classic!"

Aboard Skipum Wharf Space Station, Agresh Quadrant

It didn't take long for either ship to get clearance to dock, and they managed to take up their positions without a problem. The crew disembarked onto the docking bay and made their way through the empty corridors completely unchallenged. The people they did pass seemed completely nonplussed by them being heavily armed, probably on account of the aura the team gave off of being on military business.

"Probably just assuming we're the authorities," Sean whispered over their private comm channel.

"We *are* the authorities," Molly countered quickly just before a pair of Ogg crew members came within earshot of their group.

Apart from Pieter and Crash, the others were out en masse, moving swiftly down the corridors, weapons still in holsters. Even Brock had felt confident enough to venture out on this mission, much to Joel's surprise.

"Okay, ladies," Nickie announced over their implants. "I've got eyes on them."

Karina slowed her pace, nearly tripping Joel up behind her. "How the hell does she have eyes on them?"

Sean pulled her back into formation. "I have no eye dear," he chuckled quietly. "Get it? Eye dear…"

Karina raised one eyebrow at him, unimpressed.

"Okay," Sean conceded, making sure they maintained their position in the group sweeping the corridors. "She has implants and little marble sized devices that she can send out."

Molly and Joel turned to look at him.

"Probably," he added.

Molly had already shifted her attention back to the task at hand. "When this is all done we're going to sit down and you're going to tell me everything you know about this girl and her family."

Sean shrugged. "Well, some of it is classified."

Karina glared at him, as if with a warning.

"Oh, but I'll tell you everything you need to know, baby," he added hurriedly.

Joel noticed that Molly had heard the comment but chosen to ignore it. – at least for the time being. "Okay, focus people, we're getting close. Move in on my mark only."

He made hand signals and the team moved forward on the warehouse segment Oz had pinpointed for them as they had docked.

Jack took the initiative and moved around to flank the other side. "I'll find another door in, just in case they try to run," she told Joel quietly as she moved off.

"Good thinking, Jack," he shot back, distracted by instructing the others.

"All part of the training," she whispered through the holoconnection as she rounded the corner at the far end of the corridor they were on.

"Brock, stay close behind me," Joel continued. "Molly, if you'd like to do the honors you can go ahead. Sean and Karina, if you could fan out around the left-hand side as we breach, you can limit their options as we close in. All get into position. On my mar—"

Before Joel could give another instruction, there was an almighty bang followed by a whistling like a high-pressured kettle. Then an explosion.

The corridor shook.

"What the fuck?" Sean yelled.

Joel and Molly looked at each other. "I guess Nickie wasn't waiting around," Joel surmised.

Forced to make their move, Molly stepped up and kicked open the double door in front of them. She moved swiftly in, weapon drawn and sweeping the area for targets.

The team followed quickly behind her, entering just in time to see Nickie drop a dozen burly Leath single-handedly with rapid laser fire.

Once they were down, she busied herself, tying them up with some kind of leashing device that allowed her to hogtie each one in a matter of seconds.

The dust from the explosion started to settle, revealing a bunch of broken up crates. Crates that had been full of what looked to be spare parts. Nickie finished binding the fifth Leath and then straightened up, stretching her back like she'd been doing something mundane like cleaning.

"Anyone wanna help me get these SOBs packed away?" she asked, as the Sanguine Squadron stood around, mouths agape, and weapons still unholstered.

Molly was the first to respond. "I thought we said no killing?"

"I didn't kill any of them!" Nickie protested. "Set to stun, see?"

"And the explosion?"

"A distraction," she explained simply, kicking at some of the debris near a flaming pile of wooden pallets.

Molly put her sidearm back into her thigh holster. "Well, in that case, sure, show me that device you're using, and I'll give you a hand."

Sean looked butt-hurt. "But you said she was to wait for your mark!" he protested.

"I did," Molly agreed, turning the new toy over in her hands and then aiming it at the wrist of a downed Leath Nickie was holding up for her.

Molly fired it, and the plastic thread wrapped the wrist, leaving the other part dangling looking for the other one. Nickie dropped the bound wrist and then put the other one near it and finished the job by wrapping it with the loose thread which seemed to constrict until it held the two hands tightly behind the Leath's back as he lay unconscious on his belly.

Molly ducked as three small metal marbles, probably the ones that Sean had mentioned returned to Nickie, hanging in mid-air just a few feet from her. She swiped them out of the air with one hand, clipping them nonchalantly back into her belt. "Dunno what you're so bothered about," she commented. "I just did all your dirty work for you."

She dusted some debris from her shoulder.

Molly shrugged in Sean's direction. The rest of the team had started poking around the carnage that remained.

"Okay, let's get the weapons moved off the ship," Molly announced, handing the binder to Brock to take over.

Nickie brightened. "I'll go get my house bots. Save us getting sweaty hauling those crates."

She headed off back the way she had come, stepping over the metal door she had blasted through.

Joel sidled up to Molly. "You sure about this?"

Molly paused, then nodded. "Yeah. She's got a game plan, we just need to keep them from getting back to the Leath authorities. I'll have a chat with her before she goes, though. Sean, Karina, wanna make sure the dock is secure. Don't want any unexpected surprises."

"Yes, boss. On it," Karina called, heading out after Nickie.

I'll put the call into the Leath authorities.

Thanks, Oz.

Molly stopped to survey the scene. It sure was good to have a highly competent team, she mused to herself as she noted the sheer mess that they were going to leave behind.

CHAPTER FOURTEEN

Cyber Communications Department, Spire, Estaria

"We've been on this rotation for nearly a week," Hughes complained. He glanced over at his partner Riley. She sighed but didn't answer. He always thought of her as a tough version of prom queen. A prom queen who had no interest in dalliances anymore, and instead did her best to define herself through her work.

Riley closed the holoscreen she was using to spy into the window of the mocha shop where their target had been sitting for the last twenty minutes of her lunch break. A strand of dark hair fell against the side of her face, and without really registering she hooked it back behind her ear.

"You know the score on these things," she told him. "We sit here until the brass tells us not to." She turned to notice him. "Besides, it's a damn sight cushier than a ton of the assignments we could be on. Especially after, well, you know."

Hughes sighed, the back of his head hitting the headrest in mild frustration. "Yeah, I know." He rustled a plastic bag. "You want a sandwich?"

She shook her head. "No thanks. Hang on." She pulled up the holo again. "Okay. She's on the move."

Hughes hurriedly screwed up the bag of food and stuffed it into the side pocket of his door. He gently started the engine just in case they needed to move.

"Shit, I can't see anything from this far away. Let's get closer. Just in case."

Hughes rolled the car out into traffic with the goal of doing a drive-by whilst the target got into the imagined safety of her vehicle. Once she was inside, she would be sheltered – from most things, at any rate. Then he could turn around in a side street and follow her back to the government building secure parking lot where he would sit for another five hours until she finally finished work. Then he would follow her home where she would prepare a holoscreen dinner and crash around midnight.

"Okay. I've got her," his partner told him, her eyes scanning the holo amplification for any signs of a threat.

Hughes drove as slowly as he could without drawing attention. If he timed it just right Carpe would be in her car just as they passed her.

"She's going for the car," Riley told him.

A car pulled out in front of him, pulling his attention. "Shit, I've lost her," Riley cursed.

Then there was a scream and a flurry of activity on the street just around Carpe's car. Before he knew it, Riley was out of the car and running across two lanes of traffic, flashing her badge as if it would protect her from getting run over.

Hughes expected the worst. He pulled the car over and flew out, following his partner across the street.

He arrived panting, to see Riley pushing people back using her badge as a forcefield. "Get down, move back," she yelled. "Police! Move *back*!"

She kept turning, looking at the rooftops.

151

Hughes turned his attention to the upper windows across the street, searching for any sign of a sniper. The crowd was still in danger. *They* were in danger. Plus, there was still a chance—

He glanced down at Carpe. The bullet had gone straight through her head.

"Okay," he corrected himself. "There is no chance she's still alive."

He made a snap decision. "I'll go after the shooter," he told Riley.

She nodded her agreement. "Be careful!" she shouted after him.

He vaguely heard her as he rushed back across the street, barely aware of the sound of horns chastising him for getting in their way.

His thoughts were on other things, like exit routes a sniper might take out of a building. From the position of the body, he guessed the shot came from the red brick building directly across the street. He could be wrong, of course. That would all come out in the investigation. *Would be nice if that investigation included extracting a confession from the son of a bitch that just tapped his ward though.*

His brain scrambled, his eyes searching for a likely exit route. *Round the back,* he thought. *Too many cameras on this side of the street.* He noticed the red brick building was a hotel. That would mean security cameras in the corridors – probably.

He found the nearest alley that would let him pass behind the building and ran as fast as he could. There was a gate at the bottom. He looked around for something to help him scramble over it. There was nothing.

Then he heard the footsteps moving briskly on the other side of the gate. He pressed his face against the gate, the mesh scoring his skin, creating a hatched print. He caught sight of a figure and strained to get a closer look. The figure was dressed in black, about 6′ 2″, medium build, but definitely packing some muscles under his black atmosuit. Not only that, but he carried a large holdall. Certainly one big enough for a rifle.

Hughes was about to shout out but stopped himself. He reached for his weapon. That wasn't going to help at this angle either. He pulled his holo out. The man was walking in the opposite direction. He didn't have a shot of his face. He snapped a few images.

Now is the time to shout out, he told himself. He felt his voice get caught in his throat as the urgency of the situation caught up with him.

"Hey!" Nothing. The sound wasn't loud enough.

"Hey, you!"

That was louder.

The man turned briefly, allowing Hughes to take a snapshot of his face before he set off running down the street.

Gotcha, he thought, checking the image. It wasn't perfect, but it was probably enough to get a facial rec off the system. He uploaded it immediately, just in case anything happened, and then started heading back to help his partner out.

They were going to be in some shit for this, but at least they had a lead they didn't have before. He shook his head at how cold he had become. No more sitting watching Dorota and her holoscreen dinners. He felt bad for the old girl.

Conference room, Special Task Force Offices, Undisclosed location, Estaria

The next morning tensions ran high as the agents assembled for their briefing.

"Bravo team!" Carol called out, without waiting for everyone to settle down. "What can you report?"

Her eyes were bloodshot and puffy from lack of sleep. It was probably safe to assume that she had been up all night since getting the call, working the case leads and simultaneously keeping the higher-ups in the loop so they didn't do anything that might tie their hands in the wider investigation.

Elroy stood hurriedly, pulling up slides of data on the main holoscreen. Dhashana's head was down fielding incoming intel on her own holo. Even Cleavon looked frazzled, his shirt unironed and unstarched.

The first image on the screen was a photograph of the murder scene, showing the road and the building where the sniper shot from. "Our ward was taken out by a sniper as she came out of the Department of Cyber Communications building. The agents on the ground were unable to stop it even though they were parked just across the road. In fairness to them, it's worth noting that there was nothing they could have done – given that we were allowing Carpe to go into her place of work."

There was an awkward pause before he continued. "While Agent Riley secured the scene, Agent Hughes went after the shooter, estimating where he might be seen emerging. He managed to snap an image of the man we believe is responsible."

The next slide on the presentation showed a series of images of the shooter, dressed in black, carrying the holdall.

"We've run facial recognition. It appears that this is our guy, except we've no identity for him. He is, however, wanted in connection with a series of suspicious events. Darfort, the Engleton bombing two years ago. There are shootings going back twenty years we can connect him to." He gestured in the direction of Bates. "Even our esteemed leader has worked a case where this man was a suspect. But we've yet to obtain fingerprints or a single sample of DNA."

Dhashana's attention was back on the briefing. "Each time he strikes it seems like he just picks up and disappears until the next time. No cyber trail, no money trail, no nothing."

Carol pulled herself closer to the table on her antigrav chair. She studied the two agents who had spoken so far. "This is true," she admitted. "We nicked named him Sneaky Steve. We could never get an ID on him or tie him directly to anything. But now we know he's involved. Arnold Sloth is involved. Our job now is to find a tangible link between the two and bring them both in. We need these men taken off the board. They are both to be considered armed and highly dangerous."

She glanced at Cleavon who was taking notes on his holo. "We've been trying for a long time to get Sneaky Steve, and data analysis has always been a bottleneck. As you know, our technological capabilities are now greatly improved. Our best course of action now is to use these enhanced capabilities to find the links we need to locate them." She focused on Bravo team. "Your job is to follow communications and money trails. Find anything and everything that might be useful in finding out who these men are working for, and where they are. As soon as you have anything, you're to report to me. Is that clear?"

"Yes, ma'am," they chorused.

Cleavon raised his hand. "Ma'am, there is still the issue of the other ward. Suedemann."

"Take him into protective custody and get him into a safe house. We may need him later."

Cleavon actioned the order immediately, tapping a message to the agents who were watching Suedemann.

"Anything else?" Carol asked.

No one else dared mention anything. Raza and Soraya knew they should just get on and help Bravo team. They didn't need to be told about that.

Alisha and Joshua glanced at each other. They knew that their investigation was going to tie up with the Bravo team assignment anyway. They just needed to crunch some data. Rhodez knew what he needed to do too.

There was a flurry of activity as Carol dismissed them all, and the agents filed out of the room.

They all knew it was just a matter of time before the facial rec system would give them a location on Sneaky Steve – and then all hell would break loose.

They needed to be ready for it.

CHAPTER FIFTEEN

Special Task Force Offices, Undisclosed location, Estaria

Nearly a whole day had gone by when the alert went out. Sneaky Steve had been spotted heading into a motel on the east side of the city, miles from where the shooting had taken place.

Joshua glanced down at the alert on his holo. He knew exactly what it was before he even read it. The fact that everyone's was going off at once meant only one thing.

They were sending in a SWAT team. He opened the message. He'd been selected to attend. One look at Alisha told him she was heading out too.

The pair moved, along with another half dozen teammates toward the doors from the office. Protocol dictated that they head down to the locker rooms, change, and then head out to the weapons locker where they would be collected and taken to the location.

The excitement pumped his body full of adrenaline. He would be ready. They'd run the routine several dozen times in training, but this was the first time they would be doing it for real.

Alisha looked pale, but her eyes were wide. "I'm beginning to regret that second mocha I had this afternoon," she whispered to him as he held the door for her.

"You'll be fine," he reassured her. "Just a walk in the park."

She smiled, hurrying ahead to catch the elevator that would take them further into the labyrinth.

Rhodez watched the chosen few leave and sat back down in his console chair. He hoped they'd do okay. Whether he was there with them or not, he wanted them to win. He just realized that if he wasn't there, he couldn't influence things. He couldn't protect anyone. Specifically, Alisha. He would just have to trust that Joshua was sufficiently motivated.

Morðingi Motel, East side, Spire

The truck doors opened and the agents piled out on the street, creating a trickle of armored bodies that parted and flowed in two different directions around the motel, most to the front, some to the back.

Joshua followed behind the body he knew to be Alisha. If there was any rearrangement in order, though, it would be difficult to know who was who between the heavy gear, impaired vision of the helmets, and general confusion that always went along with these busts.

"The last sighting of our target was twenty minutes ago from a traffic cam on the other side of the street. He is checked in under the name of Hermit Rogers." Carol Bates was in every agent's ear – no doubt sitting watching everything from the tactical support vehicle that was already on location when they arrived. Joshua had clocked it just a few hundred feet up the street.

"When you're all in position I will give the go-ahead. You go on my mark and not a second before, agents."

Joshua felt weird not answering her with a 'yes, ma'am.' Given their location, Alisha was going to be the one to make the breach.

He didn't know if he should offer to do it for her. He didn't know whether that would insult her, or if she was nervous about being the one on the sharp end. But then, he reasoned, he would be more likely to kick the door down in one go. That would give them the element of surprise and keep them all safer.

He ran up the stairs double time. One of the agents in front of him had taken the motel owner aside and presumably out of the front door, pumping him for intel all the way.

In no time at all they were outside the door. 112. This was it.

Alisha stood aside. She was breathing heavily, her goggles steaming up slightly. It was time to act. The other agent in front of him stood back as well. Looks like they all agreed he was kicking it down.

He moved into position, checked that Alisha was ready and then swung forward. With the first kick the door moved under his foot but didn't break, either at the lock or at the point of impact.

More welly, he told himself.

He swung forward and kicked it again, this time as hard as he possibly could. The door frame snapped, splintering. He pushed into the weak point again and then got out of the way, allowing Alisha to trample over the top of the broken wood into the room. Her weapons were held firmly outstretched, sweeping the room for any signs of life and movement.

She stopped suddenly mid sweep to the left.

She'd found her target.

The second agent was already in after her, also moving to the left. Joshua waited a moment, and then followed the two in, covering off the space on the right-hand side of the room.

They had him.

He heard Alisha call it in over the holo.

"Okay, take him," Carol's voice commanded in their audio pieces.

"Wait, wait!" the man protested. He wore normal indoor

clothes, but there was no doubt he was the man they'd been studying from the holo image all afternoon. He moved from the left of the room, toward the window. Joshua's eyes scanned the area to see if there was a way he could use the window to escape. They were only on the first floor. Even if he jumped backward he would live.

"I can tell you things," the man continued. "You want to know who I work for right? I have evidence on all of them. On what they're plotting. *Everything.* I can—"

Alisha had left her comm open so that Carol could hear everything. Carol interjected. "Take him!" she repeated.

Joshua felt Alisha's hesitation.

And then there was a loud bang.

The man stopped suddenly, his expression changing before he fell. Joshua moved forward, looking at Alisha. Her face was frozen in shock. But he noticed her finger was still along the side of the weapon. He glanced in the direction of the body. Already there were other agents filing into the room through the broken door, fanning out, stomping, calling the word "clear" from the different rooms.

Joshua stepped forward again. The man's shirt was white, with a crimson patch growing on the back, through where the heart would have been. No exit wound though. More like the size of an entry.

Then he noticed the glass around the body.

Windowpane glass.

Then he felt the breeze. The air was coming into the room from the outside. He moved across the glass, knowing he shouldn't be disturbing it, but he was compelled.

He looked out of the window, across the street.

It couldn't be. Was it his imagination? He could have sworn he saw someone closing the window. It was difficult to see anything though. It might have been nothing.

He looked back at Alisha. She shook her head, and that told him everything he needed to know.

She. Didn't. Fire.

He muted his holo, and signalled for her to do the same. "Come on," he told her. "Let's get you some air." He made sure that the others saw him lead her out as if she were in shock for shooting someone.

He led her back out of the motel and down into the lobby. An EMT team were just heading into the building, along with any number of agents and analysts who were ready to start collecting evidence.

Or doing a clean-up.

"I didn't—" she started.

He hushed her. "I know. But that means there is someone else out there who did."

Alisha was even paler than when they had started. "We need to tell Director Bates."

"Yes. Okay. But… are you okay?"

"Yeah. Confused. But I think so," she told him.

"Okay. Go find that service truck. I think it was just up the street."

"You're not coming?"

"No, I'm going to go see if I can find out who actually shot our target."

Alisha tried to grab his wrist, but he had already taken off onto the street.

Joshua scanned up and down the road, trying to filter out all the activity that should be there to try and figure out what shouldn't. He thought about heading across the road and trying the alley. That was how Agent Hughes had caught Sneaky Steve. But he had a head start. From here, he could see who was going to emerge. He stepped back out of the way, against the wall of the motel building.

He waited there, out of the way of the clean-up crews and officials, watching.

Alisha banged on the truck door. For a horrible moment she questioned herself, wondering if it were just a service vehicle and not the ops van.

Then she heard movement.

The door opened, and there sat Carol Bates, a headset on and the operational device on two fingers of one hand, which would be used to control the specialist equipment, allowing her to zoom in, or replay at the twitch of a muscle.

"Get in," Carol told her briskly, glancing around to see if anyone was watching them.

Alisha hauled herself in and Carol slammed the door closed after her. "What's the problem, Agent?"

Alisha felt the adrenaline shock her anew. "Sorry to bother you ma'am but I thought you should know. I wasn't the one to take the shot. The target was hit by a sniper outside."

Carol frowned. For a second Alisha was sure there was a flash of recognition across her face. But then it was gone. "You mean you didn't follow the order?" Carol asked pointedly.

"No, ma'am. I hesitated. I thought you should know in case there is something else going on that we didn't know about."

Carol busied herself with the array of open holoprojectors, carefully ticking off a checklist as if wrapping everything up. Eventually she stopped and turned to the agent stooped awkwardly in front of her. "I think you need to consider your report carefully. Disobeying a direct order in the heat of the moment doesn't bode well for a long career in the department... if you understand me."

Alisha shuffled back half a step, confused. "You mean, you want me to lie on my report?"

Carol shrugged deliberately. "I'm just saying, if your report says anything other than you pulled the trigger, you should know that that would require me to order a course of psychological tests and probably months of therapy."

"But, that would mean the end of my career in the field," Alisha protested.

Carol pursed her lips. "I know. So think hard, Agent."

Alisha frowned. "But when they find the bullet...?"

"They will find it was fired from the appropriate service weapon."

There was an awkward pause. Carol returned her attention to her screens.

"You know who did it," Alisha realized.

Carol stopped again, and this time responded in a voice so low Alisha could barely make it out. "We couldn't risk this target getting away. And you *did* hesitate, Agent Montella."

Alisha suddenly understood. It was just back up. So Carol knew about it. So lying on an official report was all right, then. "Right. Okay. I'll get my report done before I go home," she promised.

"Thank you, agent."

"Yes, ma'am." Alisha tugged at the handle to the door and let herself out, back into the bustling real world, unsheltered by the sanctity of the ops van.

She needed to talk to Joshua. He needed to know. Apart from anything, she really didn't want to be doing anything off-book without at least looping him in on it. Besides, he might have some last words of advice for her, ones that could stop her from going through with it...

Outside the Morðingi Motel, East side, Spire

Hans exited out into the back alleyway, the sound of sirens filling the air as more reinforcements showed up. Red and blue flashing lights penetrated even the daylight, illuminating the area for anyone who happened upon the scene.

His job was done, and now he needed to get out of there. Not that anyone was going to be looking for him. It was doubtful anyone even realized that he was the one that delivered the death blow. Apart from maybe the agent who was supposed to have pulled the trigger. She was probably confused.

He re-ran his view through the scope in his mind's eye. There was no doubt in his mind that it was Alisha. But as long as she played along, there was nothing for anyone to worry about. They were just taking down a dangerous killer.

And yet, there was an unsettled feeling in his stomach.

He opened his holo and connected a call. A male voice answered. "It's done," Hans told him simply.

"Good. I'll tell you when it's safe to come in."

"Yes sir," Hans responded, before hanging up the call.

He hurried past the gap in the alley which led down to the street. He caught a glimpse of the police and the SWAT team. It was time to get well away from here as fast as he could.

Joshua's eyes never left the gap in the alley. He had a fifty-fifty chance of seeing the shooter leaving the building. Half the probability said he'd turn the other way. The other half said he'd leave past this side street.

He was just beginning to think his guy had gone the other way when he saw a figure. Normal passers-by would slow their walk or turn to see what the commotion was about.

This figure didn't. He just kept walking, as if in a hurry. In a hurry and dressed all in black.

It was too obvious, was it not? he mused to himself. Then, just at the last second, the figure turned and stole a glimpse in the direction of the noise.

He didn't have time to get his holo up, but there was no doubt in his mind he knew who the figure was. It was Hans Duo, their classmate—and now teammate. The one that got the special assignments with the director's husband. The one that seemed to get special treatment in the university. The one that came to them through unconventional means.

His heart skipped a beat as the realization hit him. *Hans must have been the shooter!*

He needed to find Alisha, and fast. For one thing, she needed to know that there really was another shooter.

For another, they needed to find out why Hans was in position, and they weren't told.

Something certainly wasn't right.

His eyes surveyed the scene, looking for any signs of Alisha returning from the van. It took a few minutes but eventually he spotted her and made his way through the chaos.

They needed to talk.

Special Task Force Offices, Undisclosed location, Estaria

Joshua arrived back at his desk to collect his street jacket. Alisha was already there working on her report. Her hair was still wet from the post-op shower she'd taken in the locker room. All the other consoles were empty, and even the lights in the conference room and director's office were off.

"You gonna finish that tonight?" he asked.

She glanced around to make sure they were alone. "Yeah, I said I would."

"When you talked to Bates?"

"Yeah."

Joshua slumped down in his console chair. "You know, I've been churning this in my mind. Why on Estaria would they put Hans onto it?"

Alisha's eyes widened in disbelief. "Right? And then why lie about it in the official report?" she added nodding at her screen.

"Maybe it looks better that it was a shot from the team that engaged?"

"Wasn't it inevitable, though?"

"Well, maybe that's the point. Perhaps it wasn't. I mean, if he weren't a threat, we might have ended up bringing him in. He was ready to talk after all."

Alisha cocked her head. "So, then someone didn't want him talking?"

"Maybe. I wonder what he knew…"

Alisha leaned back rocking in her console chair now. "Carol had history with him."

"Well, she told us as much herself," Joshua countered, also leaning back in his console chair as they mulled the situation.

After several moments of silence Alisha leaned up again and reactivated her screen that had dimmed out. "I wonder if this is just one of those things we'll never know the full story about."

"Maybe," Joshua added, leaning forward conspiratorially. "But we have one more play."

"Oh yeah?"

"Hans," he said simply. "He's one of us. We just need to get him drunk and ask him!"

Alisha sniggered, not really taking it seriously. "Sounds like a doable plan," she told him. "But in the meantime, I'm going to get this finished and handed in."

Joshua pushed himself off from his console chair. "Right you are then. But don't stay too late. Make sure you get some proper rest."

"I will," she promised.

Joshua grabbed the jacket he had come back down for, and then ambled out of the darkened office, leaving Alisha on her own.

. . .

Bates Residence, Spire, Estaria

Carol arrived home to find Philip taking off his atmojacket. "You just got in?"

"Just now. Ordered up dinner, though."

"Great. I'm starving!" She placed her gear on the hallway floor and took off her atmojacket.

Philip disappeared into the kitchen, calling back to her. "How about I get a bottle of something open and we can regroup and assess our next move."

Carol paused. "Next move?"

"Yeah," he called. "You don't think this is over, do you?"

She sighed. "No. You're right. Let me go change. I'll be right there."

She heard the cork pop out of the bottle. Just the sound of it lifted her spirits. She peeled her boots off and placed them on the boot rack before padding up the stairs.

When she re-emerged, she found Philip flicking through his holo messages in the sitting area. The bottle of wine stood invitingly on the mocha table, a glass already poured for her next to it. She took her place and picked up the glass, pushing her nose into it.

Philip looked up from his work, and glass in hand raised it to her. "To an operation well done, and a foe finally caught."

She smiled. He understood what a big deal this was for her. She raised her glass back to him and then took a sip. She felt his eyes on her.

"What is it?" He asked.

She sighed, placing the glass back down, contemplating her response. She took a moment before she answered. "I heard over the comm that he was willing to tell us everything. He was going to give up the whole network. Everyone he'd ever worked for."

Philip nodded, seemingly unaffected by her dilemma. "You think that we could have trusted any intel he gave us?"

She shrugged.

"At best, it would have been bogus. At worst it could have got agents killed."

"You think he had traps in place?"

"A smart guy like that? Undoubtedly."

"But if he was looking for a deal…"

Philip took another sip of wine and checked his holo. "I think it's safe to say he was only trying to save his life. You made the right call. Did you handle the agent?"

She nodded. "Yes. She came to me afterward."

"And she's going to play ball?"

"I think so."

"Good," Philip concluded. He could see his wife wasn't convinced. "Come on, we've been after him for decades. It's far better he's taken out of the picture than risk him getting out again."

"You think he'd be able to escape?"

"I think the people he works for are powerful enough to disappear him and put him back on the streets."

Carol took a deep breath, as if resigning herself to dropping the doubts she'd been battling with since the incident. "Well, probably for the best then. Though I would have liked to be able to trace this thing further up the chain."

"Me too," he agreed. "But we have agents sweeping his known safe houses and possessions for any shred of intel we can find. We might get lucky."

"Here's to getting lucky then," she said, more brightly now. She winked at him. He grinned. Just then the doorbell buzzed.

"That will be the food!" he declared, jumping up and placing his glass carefully back on the mocha table. "You wanna eat here or at the kitchen counter?"

"Here!" she called after him. "I can't move now…"

"Your wish is my command…" he called back, opening the front door.

CHAPTER SIXTEEN

Aboard Skipum Wharf Space Station, Agresh Quadrant

The gang stood around the main corridor of the Leath ship by the cockpit.

"Ok, that's the last of them," Nickie declared, glancing smugly around the Sanguine Squadron who had effectively been kicking their heels since they disembarked *The Empress* just under an hour earlier.

The last of her 'house-bots' as she called them carried the final crates of weapons from the Leath ship.

"Good. Leath authorities will be here shortly," Molly told her.

Bang bang bang.

The door to the cockpit rattled and reverberated.

"Angry old buggers, these Leath," Nickie commented, nodding at the cockpit door.

"Something tells me they don't like being confined to their own ships," Molly muttered. "I wonder if they were able to communicate with the others before we breached."

Nickie shook her head. "Nah. Meredith shut down their comm long before I launched the first missile. They've no idea what's going on, *or* what kind of trouble they're in."

Molly chuckled. "That'll be a nice surprise for them then when the authorities show up to take them into custody."

"Love to be a fly on this wall," Nickie said, patting the door of the cockpit before heading out down the main walkway. "Anyway," she added, "speaking of, authorities aren't my cuppa tea. Mind if I disappear?"

"Sure. Lemme walk you to your ship." Molly clamped a hand down on Nickie's shoulder.

Nickie glanced at the hand on her opposite shoulder and realized that this wasn't a friendly escort. This was going to be a *business* conversation.

Sean and Karina watched from the docking bay as Nickie and Molly headed past them, following the last of Nickie's crate-carrying house-bots.

Molly spoke into her holo. "Joel?"

"Yep?"

"I'm heading over to Nickie's ship. Meet you back at *The Empress* in five. Have everyone ready to leave."

"Acknowledged."

She closed the holo connection and they kept walking. Molly waited until she'd put some distance between them and the crew before she spoke again.

"So, here's the deal," she said, in a serious but semi-friendly voice. "I'm putting my ass on the line letting you take these weapons. If these resurface anywhere and the Federation find out about them, and they will, I'm *screwed*."

Nickie looked at her in protest, but Molly held up a hand silencing her.

"These weapons will not be seen again. Do you understand me?"

Nickie nodded.

"And if they are, and I get hauled over the coals, so-help-me-ancestors, I will hunt you down and rain hell on you. Understood?"

"Yes, ma'am," Nickie assured her before breaking out into a grin. "You know, you're not so bad after all," she beamed. "You talk my language, lady. We should work together again some time."

Molly chuckled, despite the inference. "Not any time soon, I hope."

"Yeah, yeah. You had a great time," Nickie argued. "I can tell."

They arrived at the dock where Nickie's ship was waiting for her.

"Bye, Nickie," Molly said, the banter subsiding. "Stay safe. And maybe make an effort to call in on your family some time. I'm sure that no matter what happened they'll be pleased to hear from you."

"Yeah. I'm sure," she responded, strutting off after her newly acquired cargo. "Laterz, alligators!" She waved her hand, then glanced back over her shoulder with all the cockiness of youth and her artificial enhancements.

Molly shook her head, watching her leave. "Kids," she muttered.

Aboard *The Empress*, Agresh Quadrant

"So? Any problems?" the General asked, noticing the rather public setting of their call in the cockpit.

Pieter and Brock sat behind Molly pretending to be working. Joel looked absorbed with the mapping console, but he too was probably just eavesdropping.

"No problems at all, sir," Molly reported. "We left the Leath for their authorities to collect them. No serious injuries on either side and the weapons have been disposed of. Your friends are in the clear."

Lance hesitated, about to correct her, but then thought better of it trying to explain himself in front of the others. "Very good," he said instead, shoving the end of his cigar in his mouth.

He narrowed his eyes suspiciously. "Anything else I should know?"

Molly seemed to falter for only a brief moment. Then she made a deliberate thinking face. "I don't think so…?"

The General paused, waiting to see if she was going to change her mind. She didn't. "Okay. Good job, Bates – and team," he added, glancing around at the others visible on screen in the cockpit. "Carry on."

"Yes, sir. Thank you, sir."

The call ended.

Joel immediately spun round in his console chair. "So, those weapons that you completely glossed over and gave to the girl who has some weird-ass relationship with the Federation. What is she going to do with them?"

Sean arrived in the cockpit just in time to answer the question, as if he'd been waiting for the conference call to finish. He plonked himself down in the console chair next to Joel. "Probably use them as bait. Lots more Skaines to clean up out in the western front."

Molly and Joel looked at him.

"I'm guessing," he said shrugging.

"You're more than guessing," Molly insisted this time. "What do you know?"

"Nothing. Specifically. She just reminds me of someone I used to know."

Molly thought for a moment, replaying her long conversation with Nickie in the conference room back at the base. "Her Aunt Tabitha. You *knew* her."

"Maybe," he said, winking. Then, as if he'd only come to stir the pot of mystery and intrigue, and gloat that he knew more than they did, he stood up and strode back out of the cockpit leaving them wondering.

Molly shook her head and put her hands on her hips. She looked at Joel exasperated.

"I got nothing," he confessed, chuckling.

Special Task Force Offices, Undisclosed location, Estaria

The following morning Director Bates strode into the meeting room from her office next door. As she entered the room her group of agents got to their feet. There were holo-screens out all over the table and presentation slides cued up on more than two agents' holos.

"Greetings of the day, agents," she addressed them, taking her seat at the head of the table and signaling they should sit too.

"We've had a win," she started. "A very good win. Congratulations to all who were there. Every single one of you assisted in us taking this threat off the board, and you should all be very pleased with your performance." Her eyes rested on Alisha. "All of you," she reiterated.

"But the threat isn't completely neutralized," she continued. "This is a marathon, not a sprint. We still have the fixer out there somewhere, and Suedermann in custody. Our best intelligence tells us that they will still try and get to Suedermann."

Joshua raised his hand. "Do we think that Sloth will try and come after him himself?"

Hans leaned forward and spoke up immediately. "Unlikely. We've never known him to do the killing himself. The clean-up, maybe."

Carol flicked her holo and a slide showing various data arrays popped up on the presentation holo. "We're running an analysis now. We're going to find Sloth and bring him in. Alive if we can. He has intel on all the pieces of the puzzle and will be a great asset if we can turn him. There will be someone coming after Suedermann. We're almost certain of that. So, for now he remains in a safe house known only to us."

She paused looking around to see if anyone else had a

ELL LEIGH CLARKE & MICHAEL ANDERLE

comment on that piece of the briefing. "Ok. What else have we got?"

Soraya raised her hand, and then pulled up a presentation slide showing more data. "The system has come back online and has found some more data ties between Sneaky Steve and Sloth. We're running them down for any possible location he might return to."

Carol pointed to her. "Good. Good investigative work." She looked around. "Anything else we should all know about?"

There were no other hands. Clearly the agents were still scrambling to figure out what the next things were they needed to act on their threads of the investigations that were still open.

"Okay, one other point of business as we're entering a transition stage between cases." Her attention fell on Cleavon who had completely zoned out of the meeting. "Mr. Cleavon Baham."

The Estarian jerked himself out of his daze, his eyes wide at being called upon unexpectedly. "Yes, ma'am."

"Your activities haven't gone unnoticed." Carol's voice was hard and commanding. Alisha stole a glance at Joshua to see if he knew what was coming. A pang of guilt rose within her. She'd been pulling Cleavon off the cases to help with their analysis. She'd put him in the cross-hairs. And here he was about to pay the price. She watched, like an observer being forced to watch a car accident.

Carol continued. "You did some excellent work back here at the base supporting your colleagues out in the field. No successful team is composed solely of superstars and front-runners. Effective teams have a range of talented people with different skills who know what they have to contribute and work like crazy to make sure that the team succeeds. You have been that person, Mr. Baham, and as a thank you I'd like to give you the opportunity to move over to Charlie team where you can continue to do the excellent work you've been doing without the obligations of field work."

Alisha leaned over to Joshua. "They're taking him out of the field?" she hissed. Joshua raised a finger from his hand resting on the table, telling her to hang on.

Cleavon's face seemed to be a mix of emotions. After a moment he looked up at Carol and grinned. "Thank you, Director Bates. That's fantastic news." There was a sigh of relief in the meeting room and a small applause in congratulations. Rhodez who happened to be sitting to his left clamped him on the shoulder and congratulated him, and Cleavon managed to lock eyes with Alisha. He beamed at her and mouthed the word "thank you" with a thumbs-up.

Alisha felt her insides relax. It seemed he was genuinely pleased.

"Okay agents," Carol called to them over the chatter. "You've done a good job. Spend the rest of today getting caught up with paperwork and plan your team's next course of action. I want reports on my desk by the end of lunch, and we'll debrief this evening with next steps. Dismissed."

The agents in the room gathered up the various holoscreens they'd left out in case they needed them to justify what they had been doing. They folded away screens and notes on their holos, and with a clatter emptied out from the room.

Joshua caught up with Alisha at the bottom of the steps into the bullpen and pulled her to one side so they couldn't be seen from the offices. "Hey," he began, grabbing her gently by the elbow. "I take it from the fact that there were no other significant changes to our team that your report said exactly what she wanted it to say then?"

Alisha smiled, acknowledging the remark without saying anything. She noticed Cleavon walk past them down the aisle. "Hey, you know what? You still owe Cleavon drinks."

Joshua started to roll his eyes.

"Hey, no," she protested. "Fair is fair, we promised him. Now it looks like it's a combined 'welcome to the team' deal."

Her eyes rested on Hans who had already headed straight back to his console over the other side of the room. "I think this is also a perfect opportunity for us to get some answers from Mr. Elusive, too."

Joshua followed her gaze. "Ok. You invite him. I'll get Cleavon and Rhodez on board."

Alisha put out her fist for him to bump her. He did, and the two parted, crossing paths to their relative marks as if choreographed in a music video.

Alisha kept Hans directly in her sights as she approached his console. "Hey," she greeted him, as casually as she could. He glanced up briefly and then carried on his work. "Hey," he acknowledged.

"I was wondering…" She paused, waiting for him to look up.

"Uh-huh?" He didn't shift his gaze from his screen.

She continued. "We're all going out for drinks later. You should join us."

There was a long pause. Alisha stood her ground, looking directly at him as if willing him to respond. His eyes stopped scanning whatever it was he was reading. "Erm. Okay. It'll have to be later though. I have a meeting at six."

Alisha felt another wave of relief. She hated the thought of not even being able to persuade a teammate to come out with them. "Well, okay then," she beamed. "We'll be at the Admiral when you get done."

Hans looked directly at her. "I'll see you there then."

Alisha wasn't sure, but there was something in the way he looked at her. It was as if he was either onto her, or he was flirting. What really bugged her was that she couldn't tell which. She gave him a quick smile and then strode away as confidently as she could.

Never let them see you squirm, she reminded herself from basic training in eliciting human intelligence.

She waited back at her console, pretending to get on with some work but replaying the moment over and over.

Meanwhile, across the bullpen, Joshua was weaving his part of the plan. "So Cleavon, we should do drinks tonight to thank you for all your hard work."

Cleavon didn't hesitate. "Awesome!" he responded straight away, the holoscreens on his wrist holo flickering and flashing all over the place, forgotten in his excitement. Rhodez turned to see what was going on.

"You should come too," Joshua called over to him. "Admiral. Straight after we finish here."

Rhodez thought for a moment before agreeing. He pushed back in his antigrav console chair. "Oh, what the heck. I can get this lot finished tomorrow. I'm in."

"Excellent," Joshua said, walking back to his desk, reveling in the sense of accomplishment that went with a good set up. *Phase 1 complete.*

Alisha gave him a thumbs-up as he approached. He returned it as discreetly as he could. The plan was afoot.

The Admiral, Spire, Estaria

The bar was a hub of activity. It was as if everyone in the nearby buildings had all gotten the idea of coming for an after-work drink at the same time.

Alisha pushed her way through the hordes of workers, trying not to lose sight of Rhodez and Joshua ahead of her. Cleavon was following her, and Hans was still in his meeting when they left the office.

"Alisha! What are you drinking?" Rhodez asked.

"Vino for me," she told him. "Thanks!"

Rhodez asked the same question of Cleavon and sent them both to try and find a table where they could stake out their claim. Alisha led the way and eventually found a tall table without seating. At least they'd be able to put their drinks down, she reasoned, as she stood by it, ready to defend it against anyone who might challenge them.

Cleavon had been chatting away over the noise for several minutes. She nodded politely, trying to hear, but really only understanding about fifty percent of what he was saying.

Eventually the other two showed up carrying their valiantly acquired drinks.

"I propose a toast," Joshua started. "A toast to our new team member Cleavon." He raised his glass, and the others followed suit. "Thank you for everything you've done for us already, and welcome to being an official part of our motley crew."

They all cheered and congratulated Cleavon. At one point Alisha was sure he had a tear in his eye. She already knew what it meant to him to be accepted and valued. She was glad they'd made the right call bringing him on board and then celebrating him.

"So, Alisha," Rhodez leaned in just a little too cozily. "Are you seeing anyone?"

Alisha froze. She knew exactly where this was going. It was almost as if it was an impossibility to go out for drinks with co-workers and for it to be purely a co-worker or platonic thing. She sighed and gave him the look. *"Really?* The first time we end up in a bar together, after a serious moment of team bonding, and *that's* what you want to ask me?"

Rhodez felt his face flush. "I'm... I'm sorry. I didn't mean to..."

Alisha rolled her eyes. "It's fine."

CHAPTER SEVENTEEN

Base conference room, Gaitune-67

It was early evening on Gaitune, and Arlene had brought Ben'or up to Gaitune for a debrief and a tour of the facility. The reasoning she had pitched to Molly was that he'd already helped them so much that he was clearly trustworthy, and having been on a mission with them he had already known about a chunk of the secret Federation technology for months and kept it to himself.

Molly had agreed, but had Oz complete a full risk assessment without letting anyone else know.

Now, seated in the base conference room with him across from her, she couldn't help but think she had been silly. There was something about his relaxed manner and sage-like wisdom that put everyone at ease. She could see what Arlene saw in him, and why he was such a good diplomat.

The meeting had already been called to order by Gareth Jones who was patched in over an advanced holoconnection. He had no idea where they all were. The connection that Oz and ADAM had engineered in the beginning between Estaria and Gaitune

ELL LEIGH CLARKE & MICHAEL ANDERLE

made it look like they could be somewhere on the planet and talking with him.

Paige and Maya sat down one side of the conference table to Molly's left, and Gareth's image sat in the middle of the table able to face each of them at the same time.

Gareth announced the good news. "Well, folks. It looks like we've done it. The university will live to fight another semester."

There was applause in the room. He continued. "We had official word today that the results of the investigation were found to be erroneous. Someone made an administrative mistake, and in light of funding cuts they're going to drop any further investigation."

Molly looked around the small team and relished the smiling faces. "This was indeed a win. Well done folks," she added. "Ben'or, we appreciate you coming in and giving us the saving guidance right at our eleventh hour. Your input is very much appreciated."

"Gareth," she said, turning to the screen. "You and your legal team have worked tirelessly to keep our survival a possibility. You have our eternal gratitude. Thank you for everything you've done."

Gareth nodded, a little embarrassed by the appreciation. "Just doing the right thing," he muttered, smiling secretly.

"Arlene, your dedication to the Academy has been second to none. I know this started as a cover for you, but everything you've done to help us stay open has been very much appreciated. Thank you."

Arlene nodded, also blushing a little now.

"Paige and Maya. I don't know where we would have been without you two. And honestly? I don't know where you each find the time to do everything that you do, on top of your normal workload. Your leadership on this issue has been inspiring, and I'm so grateful to you."

"Anytime," Paige said.

Maya grinned. "You're welcome. Though, I think we need the morning off tomorrow."

Molly cocked her head not quite understanding.

"So we can celebrate tonight," she clarified.

"Oh. Yes, of course," Molly laughed. "Absolutely! You've earned it."

Molly went back to addressing everyone in the group. "I know you've all called in favors and it's cost you social collateral. I want you to know how much we... I, appreciate everything you've done."

Paige leaned forward in her seat raising her hand from the table. "You know, we should have a celebratory party for everyone who helped us. It would be nice to thank them personally."

She and Maya exchanged a knowing look.

Gareth interjected. "I'm not sure if some of our contacts want to be drawn into something like that." He stuttered a little bit as he processed his thoughts. "Others knowing about their involvement. However. I think that is a lovely idea."

Molly grinned. "Paige, even you couldn't possibly take on planning something else at this stage. Not on top of everything else you're doing."

"Maybe I could get someone to help?" she suggested, turning her head to Maya, whose eyes lit up.

"I would be thrilled to," Maya enthused. She then mouthed the words 'thank you' to Paige.

Molly shrugged. "Sure. If Maya's up for it, we'll clear some budget for it."

There was some spontaneous chatter amongst the group for a few moments before normal business resumed. Gareth had a few things they needed to be aware of, and then Molly let the others in on a few of the moving parts they had to grease in order to make sure the investigation was dropped.

She told them it was important that they had an idea, just in case there were other signs of anything resurfacing or coming back to bite them.

She talked a little about transparency and the balance between that and keeping certain things classified. Oz agreed to act as point on any future threats that they flagged so he could make the assessment as to what was disseminated, and then after a few other comments the meeting was wrapped.

"And again, thank you, everyone!" Molly applauded. "I'll get in touch with Mom and thank her for her part too. I'll look forward to seeing you at the party, if not before."

Gareth signed off on the conference call and the others started to move.

Arlene took Ben'or by the arm. "How about we head out for dinner. Just the two of us?"

Ben'or patted her hand on his arm. "I think that's the best idea I've heard all day."

Arlene raised her eyebrows. "This coming from the diplomat who has been in strategy calls with his people all day."

Ben'or leaned down to whisper to her. "Exactly," he agreed. "So, Pods?"

Arlene flashed him her enigmatic smile. "How about we visit one of the places here on Gaitune."

"Oh, of course…you used to live here."

"Yes. A long while," she agreed. "So I know all the best places on this tiny rock."

The pair headed down the side of the meeting room toward the door.

"I think I'll see what everyone else is up to and put a food order in too," Paige started saying to Maya.

Molly interrupted Maya from responding. "Maya, have you got a second?"

Maya froze.

Paige was already almost out of the door and looked back to see what was happening. Molly caught her eye and Paige took it as a sign to wait for Maya outside. She slipped out of the door behind Ben'or and Arlene and disappeared from view.

"I'll catch you up," Maya called out to her. She hovered by the end of the table, around the corner from where Molly was still sitting. "What's up?" she asked.

Molly gave her a suspicious look. "What are you up to?" she asked bluntly.

Maya smiled sweetly. "Planning a party now it seems."

"I don't buy it."

Maya narrowed her eyes at Molly as if she were trying to suss out her line of questioning. "What's not to buy?"

Molly leaned back in her seat, closing her remaining open holoscreen. "Once an investigative journalist, always an investigative journalist," she said cryptically.

Maya's smile relaxed as if she had just been caught in a lie. "Okay, you got me. Paige and I were talking earlier, and we just figured that more intel is better than less. It would be interesting to get some of these people into a room and talk to them. Not interrogate them, but just put faces to names, press some flesh. You know."

Molly nodded, her lips turned up in approval. "Smart move," she said. She stood up.

"So that means I can? You're okay with it?"

"Of course, I am. You and Paige are the best damn investigators that I've ever known. I'm blessed to have you on my team, and I'm thrilled you're taking the initiative. You go for it. Be discreet. Try not to piss any of these contacts off, and let me know if you need anything."

Maya looked so excited Molly wasn't sure if she was about to explode. "Brilliant!" Maya said, in her best archaic accent.

Even Molly had to snigger. She wondered if she had reserved that word just for her, given her obsession with the ancient Earth shows of the little island with the funny accent.

Maya grinned. "Thanks, Molly. I'll keep you in the loop."

"I'll appreciate that," Molly replied, giving her the nod that she was dismissed.

Maya trotted out of the room and started chattering to a hovering Paige as soon as she got into the corridor.

Molly sighed happily to herself, listening to them go. Ancestors only knew what she had done to deserve to have such great people around her, but if she ever found out, she'd never stop doing it.

Special Task Force Offices, Undisclosed location, Estaria

Carol, Philip, and Hans sat in the meeting room waiting for the last of the department's agents to leave the bullpen for the night. Carol closed the door to the meeting room as Hans sat down placing a bug detector on the table.

"Are we good?" she asked.

He nodded. "We're good."

"Let's get to it then." She pulled up a holoscreen with some of the elements the task force had been working on over the past weeks. "We need to find their plan. Whatever it is that these incidents are a part of, we need to figure it out and bring a stop to it."

Hans and Philip watched in silence.

Carol leaned on the table. Her eyes burned with an intensity Hans had never seen before. "We need to figure out what the big picture is."

Philip was leaning back in his chair, with one hand on the table next to him. He turned his hand over, in a shrug like fashion. "How?"

"Well I think we need to start with what each of these positions has in common?" she explained.

Hans jumped straight in. "All positions that could influence the decisions in a department. But we knew that already."

"Yes," she agreed. "So what do the *departments* have in common? Or what use would they serve?"

Hans started plotting it out on the presentation holoscreen, moving the elements and images around from his holo as the Director and his mentor looked on.

"Robert Califray," he started. "He's our guy who disappeared on holiday. He worked in the Department of Logistics. This is the department that maintains near space satellites which are used for far communications systems." He added some notes to the board and pulled the department details to the fore.

"Then we have the Department of Near Space Communications. Malone Houston was at the Department of Off-World Logistics. This department controls outer space satellites. It's government-owned."

Philip shifted in his seat. "I've never understood why this wasn't under the military. They'd be far better funded to manage it."

Hans nodded. "I agree. But it seems that they're forced to liaise with the military because occasionally they need them. Eventually they will be transferred to a military operation."

Carol jumped in. "Yes. There's been a bill presented on it a number of times, but it's been delayed each time."

"I guess," Philip started saying slowly, formulating his thinking as he spoke, "if you wanted to influence the military or affect that network in some way, it would be easier if it were an underfunded municipal department rather than a military operation. Maybe that was why Houston was replaced?"

Hans switched the material up on the screen to reflect their working theory as it was evolving. He put word military on there too.

Carol took over listing out their remaining targets. "Then we have Goran Suedermann, our at-risk person at the Division of Holo Crimes. What do we know about this place?"

Philip shrugged one shoulder. "Well, it's a pseudo law enforcement department. It keeps the network safe from scams. You know, data protection, malware, et cetera."

"And Ms. Dorota Carpe," Carol continued. "Head of Cyber Communications, who oversees regulation of public communications."

She stared at the details on the board, tapping a finger to her lips as she thought. "Something isn't making sense."

Hans added some text to the display. "Hang on. This department is also responsible for the infrastructure of the holo network. They maintain the servers and relays for the whole planet."

Carol took a deep breath. "So what's the pattern?"

"Well," Philip said, standing up. "If you wanted to control significant aspects of the planet, and the decision making with big things as it relates to our interactions with other planets, then these are probably the most significant points to control. You can control outgoing communications, domestic communications. Media, too."

Carol took over. "As well as military ships if you were able to feed them false intel. I believe, gentlemen, we're getting a picture of what our friends at the Northern clan are planning."

Philip sat back down, his eyes fixed firmly on the screen in front of him. "Something big is coming. This feels like a preparation."

"Preparation for what though?" Hans asked.

Carol looked at the slides, her face as serious as even Philip had ever seen it. "Preparation for war."

There was a long silence in the meeting room.

Eventually Carol spoke. "Think about it. If you were waging war with an outside force these positions would allow you to control everything you needed to."

"You mean someone beyond the Sark System?" Philip interjected.

"Exactly."

"Well who?" he asked, his face gaunt and pale now. "The Federation?"

"Perhaps."

"But the Federation would kick our asses," Hans remarked seriously.

Carol spoke faster as she started to put it all together. "Not if there were allies waiting in the wings. Lance was onto this. He gave us the tips. He must know something, and whatever he planned he'll have the Federation's wellbeing at heart."

Hans's eyes lit up with the realization. "So you think that by thwarting whatever is going on here he's actually protecting the Federation."

"Exactly. Else why bother?"

The Admiral, Spire, Estaria

The rest of the evening went by without incident, and eventually Hans showed up. By that time most of the end-of-day workforce had drunk their fill and left, on account of them having lives and homes to go to.

Alisha stood up from the booth they'd acquired as the crowd had thinned. "Hans Duo! You're looking way too sober!" she insisted. "Let me get you a drink."

Hans joined her at the bar and they ordered some more drinks. "Allow me," he told her, paying for the drinks. They took their full glasses to the next booth along from the others and sat down.

"So, I heard you shot a bad guy," Hans started.

Alisha watched him as she took a sip of her wine. "I could say the same," she said coyly.

Hans allowed himself a half smile. "Well, I guess we don't have any secrets then."

Alisha didn't comment. She realized there was no point in pushing it. To ask him questions about it would only weaken her standing in the interaction.

Instead, she did what any effective operative would do in a

standoff: she changed the subject. "So, what was your meeting about to keep you from our company for so long?"

"Codeword-*Classified.*"

She glared at him playfully. "I hope this isn't how all our conversations are going to go tonight, else things are going to be pretty dull."

"You know there are things I can't tell you, just as there are things you can't tell me."

She sighed, placing her drink down deliberately on the table. "So what *can* you tell me?"

"Well," he smiled, looking past her. "I can tell you that Cleavon has a crush on you, though he doesn't know it yet."

"What do you mean he doesn't know it yet?"

"He hasn't registered it consciously, but he keeps looking over at you. Even when we were at the bar."

Alisha sighed. "Okay, tell me something interesting. Not about boys."

He paused. "The Director has her eye on you for promotion."

"Promotion? We just got here."

Hans smiled sagely over his glass. "The grooming has already begun, though. You're dedicated. You take your job seriously, and it's clearly being noticed."

"What on Estaria makes you think that?"

"I told you, I pay attention."

Alisha noticed that Hans had drunk about half of his beer by this point. Not enough to spill state secrets, but maybe enough to loosen him up a touch. "And what about *your* career? You're always off doing things separate from the rest of us, with your secret meetings with the Director after the main meetings. What are you up to?"

He shrugged. "Just doing my job."

"Which is?"

He glanced off into the crowd. She had him. "The same as you," he responded.

"Not the same as me," she told him firmly.

"Pretty much the same as you."

"You're very good at not giving anything away."

He shrugged again. "We were all taught the same techniques."

"Yet we all ended up with different skills, doing different missions."

"I guess. So tell me, what does Alisha Montella do on her days off?"

"Changing the subject," she remarked. "I see how this is."

"I can't tell you all my secrets on a first date." *He was trying to distract her,* she noted.

"This is a date?"

"Do you want it to be?"

"Again with the answering questions with questions."

"That's what you get when you date a spy."

Alisha nodded, quietly absorbing the checkmate she was advancing toward.

He kept talking to her. "You know that look?"

"What look?"

"The look you have right now. I'll bet that's the same look you put a lot of guys through when you talk your way around them."

"I don't—"

"You do," he insisted firmly. "You have a way of keeping people at arm's length while letting them think that you're being friendly."

Alisha said nothing.

"Nothing? Well, I never thought I'd see the day the great Alisha Montella had nothing to say. I should take this down as a noteworthy date in my calendar. You need another drink." He got up and headed to the bar again.

Joshua and Rhodez showed up at their booth. "Everything okay?" Joshua asked.

Alisha exhaled, frustrated, and pushed back in her seat. "Yeah. All fine."

Joshua leaned in. "You working on the, um..."

She nodded.

"Okay. Well, look, Cleavon has had too much to drink, so we're going to get him back to one of our places. You sure you're going to be okay with Hans?"

She sat up to whisper to him. "I'm still working him. He's only one drink in."

Joshua grinned as if it were all just a game. "Okay. Good luck." He hesitated a moment. "Be careful he doesn't end up working you."

Alisha grinned. "I will," she said with a tone of determination. "He's getting nothing out of me."

She waved at Rhodez propping up Cleavon just behind Joshua. He grinned and waved back. "See you at work tomorrow," he called over.

She leaned past him to address their newest team member. "Yeah. Plenty of water before you sleep, Cleavon!"

He gave her a thumbs-up and then, propped up between Rhodez and Joshua, he was escorted out.

A moment later Hans arrived back from the bar carrying a glass of wine and glass of beer. "They're leaving?"

"Yeah. Cleavon's had enough and they want to make sure he's safe."

Hans smiled. "So they're leaving you to continue grilling me about my secret off-book missions?"

Alisha tried not to show too much enthusiasm. "Ah, so you're ready to talk then?"

He silently handed her the new glass of wine without answering her question, and they clinked glasses.

CHAPTER EIGHTEEN

Base Conference Room, Gaitune-67

Molly sat in the conference room, finishing up some work.

The lights in the corridor beyond had gone off long ago, and it was just Molly's body temperature that was telling the conference room that there was someone still in there because her movements on her holo barely registered with the motion sensors at all.

It's getting late to call your Mom, Oz reminded her.

Shit. Okay. Patch me through.

A new holoscreen opened from the center of the table and folded out as a three-dimensional cube ahead of her. The setting was still on for it to display in the center of the table rather than the wall.

The call connected and the life-like, life-sized image of Carol Bates appeared in front of her. She felt a weird resistance in her stomach to have her so real in front of her after so many years of not communicating with her at all.

"Hi, Mom," she started.

Carol was clearly still at work, if the plain walls of her windowless office behind her were anything to go by.

Carol tried to smile. It didn't suit her. "Ah, you're back."

"What do you mean, 'back?'"

"You've been out of the system."

"You talked to Paige?"

"I didn't need to. My agents were trying to run advanced analysis and kept reporting that the boosted component was down."

Molly bobbed her head, understanding now. "So you knew that Oz wasn't within range."

"They didn't make me a spy for no reason." She smiled again.

"I see that."

"So, what was the mission?" Carol asked, trying to sound more Mom-like and less director-of-the-spy-agency. Molly noticed it was hard for her. Rigid, almost. She wondered briefly how she managed when she had been out in the field. How could she have persuaded assets and put them enough at ease to turn them? How could this woman have infiltrated anywhere?

Her people skills reminded her of…well, of her own.

"Mom, you know I can't tell you."

"It was a Reynolds special, wasn't it?"

"Mom!"

"Ah ha! It was. Well, I hope for your sake it went well."

Some people had their Moms grilling them about where they'd been and who they'd been out with. My Mom grills me about classified missions. Some dynamics just can't be skipped.

Indeed. Maybe she's just showing an interest.

No. She just wants to know. She's still obsessed with her little vendetta against the General.

At least they're on the same team now.

Small mercies.

"Mom, he only has the good of the Federation at heart," Molly insisted out loud.

"I know, that's what worries me. I care about my daughter."

Molly raised her eyebrows skeptically. "Which is why you remained in active service while I grew up."

Carol's face darkened. "You were perfectly safe," she insisted firmly.

"Knowing what I know now, I think that term is relative."

"What are you saying?"

"Nothing."

"Clearly something. Come on. Are you saying I was a bad mother?"

"No. I'm saying that if I really was as important as you're making out in comparison to Lance Reynolds' priorities, maybe you wouldn't have let me feel so guilty all this time for what happened when you and Dad were taken."

Carol seemed a little less in control all of a sudden. "I told you it wasn't your fault."

"Did you? Did you really?" Molly could feel the anger rising in her chest. She fought it to stay calm. The last thing she wanted was to get all upset now. There were more important things to discuss.

Carol's voice broke a little as she spoke. "Of course I did. I sat you down and I said that they were bad men that took us."

"But it was my fault the bad men showed up. I didn't have any context."

"So is that why you called me? To tell me what a shit mother I've been to you?"

"No. Actually. I called you to say thank you for doing a great job in saving the University."

There was an awkward silence on the line. Carol shifted in her seat. "Oh. You're welcome. Like I said, I wanted to do right by you and I knew how important that place is to you."

"And I appreciate it," Molly said, the emotion gone from her voice now.

Carol hesitated before broaching the next subject. "There's something else you should be aware of though, Molly."

I always get nervous when she uses my name.

I can see why...

"What's that?"

Carol leaned forward on her desk, her arms folded in front of her. "For the last couple of weeks, your grad students have been running down leads where people have been removed from specific positions of power."

"Yeah, I've been getting the reports."

"What I'm about to tell you isn't in a report. We only figured it out an hour ago. Something's coming. Lance knew it. That's why he brought me into the fold."

"What is it?"

"You're not going to like it."

Aboard *The Penitent Granddaughter*, Agresh Quadrant

Nickie paced up and down the grated walkway of the bridge. Grim watched her, his head feeling dizzy going back and forth again and again. He started to say something, but then thought better of it.

"Anything?" Nickie demanded.

No one responded.

"Meredith!" she called, lifting her voice to the intercom as if Meredith didn't already hear her every thought.

"Hang on. I may have something," Meredith told her calmly.

Nickie continued to pace.

Grim couldn't contain his comment. "You know, you're going to wear that walkway out," he said, immediately regretting it.

"Well, as soon as Meredith locates our lost Skaine ship we'll be on our way and I won't have to wait so attentively."

Grim sighed, relaxing back in the chair he'd perched on. "At least they let us take the weapons, so we can track down the Skaines."

"True," she conceded, stopping in her tracks, her hands now

on her hips. "But what are the odds? Middle of fucking nowhere and I run into these people." She shook her head, genuinely flummoxed. "I just can't believe it was an accident."

"No, the likelihood does seem pretty remote," Grim confessed.

"Unless the Federation is onto me."

Meredith interrupted. "Unlikely," she said. "They made the agreement. You had seven years."

"Yeah, but you're all activated and everything. Are you telling me you haven't transmitted my location?"

Meredith's voice remained steady. "I think we need to focus on what's happening right now."

Nickie's eyes narrowed, and Grim could see the frustration in her eyes. "Meredith, that's not answering the question."

"Well, yes," Meredith confirmed. "Technically you are traceable. But only intermittently, and they'd need to want to find you *and* be paying attention to get a lock on you. But with the way you left things, they have no reason to be looking for you."

Nickie huffed and sat down in the pilot's seat. "But those Federation-bunnies knew so much."

Grim notice her anger deflate into something else. "They made you miss home?"

Nickie's face relaxed some more, as if she was surrendering to what she was really feeling. "Made me miss Aunt Tabitha," she confessed.

Grim shuffled in his chair, his back legs uncomfortably hanging down the side of the seat. "Well given the remote chances of this happening, and the way it happened, some civilizations might call what you experienced fate."

She frowned, distracted. "What d'you mean?"

He shrugged, his eyes soft with empathy. "Well, maybe there was a reason you ended up reconnecting with some part of the old family. That's all."

There was a moment of silence. Grim tried to formulate something else to say to her. Something that might help her face her anger. Something that could help ease the pain she still clung to like a candle she kept burning for loved ones long gone but not forgotten.

"Okay. I need a drink," she declared, her tone hardening. She stood up, her boots clunking on the metal floor. "Meredith, lemme know when you have something we can work on." She strode across the bridge and headed out into the ship.

Grim shuffled awkwardly off the chair, stretching his body that had started to stiffen up. As soon as he could he followed her out, hitting the open door button just as the door had started to close behind her.

"I will," Meredith said to the empty room. "I will."

CHAPTER NINETEEN

<u>**Game Server, Base, Gaitune-67**</u>

Bourne and Oz lurked in the server they'd partitioned off for the purposes of the latest craze that had hit the Gaitune gamers: Massively Multiplayered Role Playing Game, specifically *Space Orcs vs Solari.*

"You know," Bourne mused, "there's nothing wrong with a little bit of scene-setting while we wait. So we'll be ready when they all log on."

"I suppose that's not entirely unreasonable," Oz agreed carefully, already generating Non-Player Characters, NPCs, and the space station around them. It was a multi-leveled behemoth of a station, every inch of it made of gleaming chrome and neon lights.

"I mean, it beats looking through the archives for another six hours," Bourne carried on, half of the NPCs taking the shape of the Solari faction. The Solaris displayed as thinly-disguised space elves with silver skin and armor that was intricate to the point of being impractical. "And we could try out some new tactics!" he added enthusiastically.

"I already agreed," Oz pointed out as the other half of the

NPCs took the shape of the Um'Mal faction; quintessential space orcs. They looked like the aftermath of a pair of comets meeting at high speed before tumbling into mismatched armor.

The faction leaders took form on the central platform as their armies sprang into existence throughout the space station. Terminals started sparking, windows and walls cracked, and laser fire began to fly through the air as the last details of set dressing appeared.

The Um'Mal leader let out a ferocious war cry like a meteor breaking a planet's atmosphere and lunged. A bubble shield burst into life around the Solari leader and sent the orc flying aside.

Below their platform, the rest of the station erupted into chaos; the chaos of two AIs battling it out in terrain that their friends the humans would never even see.

Base Workshop, Gaitune-67

"So, that was a clusterf—"

"We handled it." Crash cut Pieter's complaint off before he could finish. "We can handle the debriefing later and—...and no one is listening to me," he added to himself as Brock and Sean stampeded past him to the workshop.

Pieter gave him a consolatory pat on the back before loping after them with Joel at his side, leaving Crash to take up the rear at a more sedate pace.

By the time he arrived in the workshop, there was a trail of discarded gear across the floor and the space was humming with life. Sean and Brock were already moving the couch into place. It was an old, battered relic, originally a grimy beige and red tartan, though it had been patched in about fourteen other types of fabric as life gradually wore it to pieces. It probably should have been replaced half a lifetime ago, but the last time anyone had suggested such a thing Pieter and Brock had both acted as if someone were threatening to drown a puppy. Paige had put the new sofas elsewhere in the workshop, but she realized they were probably never going to be used.

Sean and Brock stopped once the couch was facing the largest stretch of flat, clear wall in the workshop. When Crash stepped farther into the room he hit the light switch reflexively, plunging the workshop into dim blue-gray light; dark save for the various monitors and equipment in the room. At least until Pieter turned on the holoscreen, the light of an unused channel spilling over the wall in front of the couch and casting everyone in stark silver.

Joel turned the gaming console on almost as an afterthought before he dropped onto the couch, slumping down into the cushions as the silver light was replaced by the 3D multicolored logo and overly chipper jingle of the console's startup routine. He held his hands out to accept the controller and Brock handed it to him, but before Brock could sit down himself Sean vaulted over the back of the couch and usurped his space. Brock spared only a moment to look affronted before sidestepping to take the next seat over.

With a grin that stretched nearly wide enough to split his face, Pieter hip-checked Brock out of the way and sat down, followed almost immediately by Crash dropping into the last available seat.

Brock scowled theatrically and planted his hands on his hips for a moment before he threw his hands up in exasperation, sharply at odds with the soothing menu music that had replaced the startup tune.

"C'mon," he groused, even as he turned away to collect the rest of the controllers. He passed them out with the air of a pouting puppy before he finally took the only seat still available to him: the floor in front of the overly crowded couch, his back against Crash's legs.

Crash set his gaming controller down on top of Brock's head in much the same way as one might use a coffee table. Brock couldn't even bring himself to protest.

It was a disarmingly homey corner, almost at odds with the rest of the high tech of the workshop—the rest of the base as a whole—but soon enough most of them would break the quiet to start jeering at each other and it would fit together with the rest of the loud, bright puzzle pieces that made up the base.

Game Server, Base, Gaitune-67

On the planet Velmark a hurricane battered a temporary colony, sending everyone within it running in every direction as they tried to batten down the hatches before the power went out. Waves crashed on beaches of coal and diamond dust and the wind tore at the prefabricated buildings as if the storm was trying to sweep the entire colony away, regardless of the people running around like an army of ants inside the walls.

Pirates boarded a cargo cruiser in the Perseus arm of the galaxy, shouting back and forth to each other as they spread throughout the ship and took all that they pleased, gathering up everything that looked valuable and leaving nothing in their wake. They left the cruiser a drifting wreck when they were done; ransacked and empty of the crew it had once held, and just waiting to be stumbled upon at some point in the future.

A duo of scout corvettes cruised low through the atmosphere of a desert world, weaving through windswept bands of red and gold sand as they just barely stayed ahead of the storm building behind them. Lightning arced through the flying sand and wind buffeted the corvettes like flies in a tornado, and the cockpits were filled with chatter as the pilots tried to coordinate with each other even though the storm's interference rendered much of what they said unintelligible with glitching static. Soon enough the storm caught up with them both, spinning them in every direction and pelting the cockpits with sand, gravel, and the occasional rock the size of a fist.

A stampede of massive deer-like anterons trampled a field

flat on the planet of Wybesal, herded toward a water trap by a trio of rednecks on jury-rigged speeders. They whooped and hollered and shouted back and forth to each other as the herd galloped closer and closer to the trap and the pasture that sprawled beyond it, and the air was filled with the anterons' trumpeting and shrieking. An older beast tripped and fell, and in single file every anteron that might have tripped on it instead leapt right over it until it struggled back to its feet and resumed running.

Two people on one planet, seven on another, a crew of dozens in a ship out in dark space, crowds of thousands in a space station filled with refugees as a colony fell out of orbit, and countless other people in countless other places, until the game world buzzed with simulated life.

"What else can we do?" Bourne wondered. Reshaping a digital world was not too difficult a task when one was a digital being who had initially been programmed for much more taxing things. It was a bit like playing at the seashore, seeing what could be made before the ocean rushed up and swept it all away in a fit of pique. "What about mercenaries?" he mused. "I suppose that wouldn't be so different from pirates, though."

"Mercenaries are being paid," Oz replied reasonably. "Pirates pay themselves after the fact."

"That is a very polite way of phrasing it," Bourne returned, almost as if he admired the phrasing. "Oh, you know, there was a thing I saw in the archives... I mean, I saw a lot of things in the archives, but this one seemed cool and we could probably do something like *that*. It wouldn't be too difficult to pull off..."

In a gleaming city that seemed to consist mostly of glass and chrome spires, a man in a mirrored cloak aimed a crossbow straight at a window. It should have been bullet proof, but that didn't mean much to the concussive crossbow bolt that smashed through it a moment later. The man dashed through the broken glass with all the grace of a cat, and once inside he began gathering as many of the possessions of the clearly wealthy inhabitants as he could until his bags and his arms were full.

Just in the nick of time as it turned out (since he could hear sirens steadily getting closer), he absconded out the same window he had used to get in, holding his treasures close. He knew quite a few people who needed it more.

"I'm pretty sure he was actually fictional," Oz pointed out, slightly dubious as the scene unfolded even as he sent the police after the thief.

Bourne scoffed, making his opinion on that statement very clear. "*So?*"

Brock made an aggravated noise as his avatar jittered in place, locking up halfway through the animation to swap out a weapon. It took almost a full minute before his avatar finally managed to complete the movement, but the pistol he grabbed was less of a gun and more just a floating cartridge before the rest of the model abruptly snapped into existence.

"Hey, Oz?" Crash called. His own avatar jogged in place before abruptly lurching forward several paces, where it then repeated the performance as if the act of running was suddenly too difficult for it to comprehend.

It continued running in place for several seconds after Crash gave up trying to go anywhere.

He got no response from the AI, and he sighed in quiet irritation before letting it go.

Steadily the games graphics degraded until Sean scoffed, "I could do better than this with my damn holocomm." As if to punctuate his words, his armor vanished for a split second before popping back into place as if nothing had happened.

The draw distance shrank until they could all scarcely see more than a few meters in every direction around their avatars;

everything beyond those few meters was a white void. Even then, the merchant standing to Pieter's left was still reduced to nothing but a set of floating teeth, partially rendered hair, and disembodied eyes before the rest of the model finally managed to render back into existence, the detail so low that its polygons were almost visible and its facial features were nearly flat.

Joel cocked his head to one side and contemplated the screen where a text box opened and closed repeatedly as he tried to end a conversation with an NPC. He pressed every button on the controller and jiggled the joysticks and finally the text box closed, only for his avatar to immediately get launched into the air—so high up that the map vanished, and he just kept going higher. Even once he started falling, it took a few seconds for his avatar to start flailing appropriately.

"Huh," he observed flatly, his expression bemused. His avatar fell for a full thirty seconds before dying on impact with the ground. "Well, that was something."

Joel tried to respawn and everything froze. He pressed a few buttons. Sean jiggled the joysticks. Crash gave his controller a shake. Pieter reached over and tapped the console.

Nothing happened; the game remained frozen.

The graphics flashed a few times and a few notes of the background music managed to come through, mixed oddly with a few mangled lines of idle NPC dialogue. And then the map disappeared entirely, leaving a few disconnected pieces of architecture floating in a white void. Nothing else happened at all after that.

"Oz?" Joel called, hoping that the first failure to get the AI's attention had just been a fluke.

Unfortunately, after a rather pregnant pause he still received no answer. Taking a different tack, he tried, "Bourne?" instead and waited expectantly, his eyebrows rising as the silence drew longer.

When he didn't get an answer from Bourne either, he sighed and reached over to reset the console.

"Seriously, what are they doing?" Brock asked, his expression twisting with confusion as he rubbed the back of his head with one hand. The vibrantly colored nails of his other hand tapped against his beer in an aimless pattern, his currently useless controller abandoned in his lap.

Without any warning, both Bourne and Oz found themselves booted out of the server as it shut down. They were midway through a police chase as every local squadron pursued the members of a smuggling ring through the air over the crystalline city of Amestria, and it all ground to a halt just as it was getting to the good part. Just as the chase fumbled into oncoming traffic, sending hover cars and personal ships lurching out of the way as they were lit with multicolored police lights, everything abruptly vanished. The silence afterwards was nearly deafening.

For a moment neither of them did anything.

Then they each rapidly ran a set of maintenance scans, just to make sure the problem hadn't been on their end. When all of the scans came back clean and clear, they probed curiously at the server once again. They were greeted with a canned maintenance message in the form of a tiny spaceman holding up a sign that said, We're sorry, the server is undergoing maintenance right now. Thank you for your patience!

Finally Bourne wondered, "You don't suppose we took it a little too far, do you?"

He tested the server again, giving a pleased, "Oh!" when he found himself back in the game. "Never mind, we're fine. I suppose they just rebooted it."

"We should maybe take that as a sign," Oz suggested, though he didn't seem particularly stern. Bourne seemed disinclined to acknowledge his words.

"Aaand we're live!" Pieter cheered as the game restarted, pumping the hand holding his beer into the air and nearly spilling it on Sean's knees. "Whoops."

"Second time's the charm?" Brock suggested cautiously, picking his controller back up. "C'mon, let's just stick together this time," he wheedled. "Maybe it won't all implode if we aren't all spread out."

"That wasn't how it worked," Sean groused, but he didn't actually offer a protest. Figuring out what was going on had rather quickly jumped up his list of priorities.

Joel chuckled to himself, amazed at what was happening. He quickly extracted himself from his squished position on the couch. "Restart. I'm going to get some more beers." He bounced up the stairs, taking two at a time with his beer bottle in hand as a mascot.

He passed Paige and Molly, who were sitting quietly in the common area, and mock-saluted them. Paige wiggled her fingers, and Molly grinned and flipped him her middle finger. He sniggered as he wandered passed, catching only a part of their conversation as he headed into the kitchen.

Empty Thai containers were strewn about the table, left over from their dinner. Maya was nowhere to be seen, but the cocktail shaker in the sink and a glass on the side told him that she'd be back at some point. He opened the fridge and located another six pack of Yollin beer.

That was when he realized that he could hear Molly and Paige talking from here.

He held his breath as he listened.

CHAPTER TWENTY

Common area, Safehouse, Gaitune-67

"So, the Federation has rogue agents," Paige sighed after hearing the rest of what had happened with Nickie.

She and Molly sat in the otherwise empty common area. The holoscreen was off, and they hadn't even put on mood music. Maya's sticky drink sat abandoned on the mocha table, as Molly nursed her third beer of the evening, and Paige sipped her second cocktail.

"Well I wouldn't say she was a rogue agent," Molly explained. "Although, she seemed to be running her own mission without direct contact or supervision from the Federation."

Paige frowned thoughtfully. "That's strange, isn't it though? You wouldn't think they'd sanction that."

Molly shrugged. "They sanctioned *us*."

"Yeah, but that's different. We run ops that they give us. We operate below the radar. We're still affiliated with them and they still supply us with ships and equipment and technology. This Nickie girl, it felt like she was out on her own, with people she just seemed to acquire."

Molly picked at the label on her beer. "I did get that sense too. Neither of them had any military training or skills."

"But man, that Grim could *cook!*" Paige squealed, becoming more animated now. "Oooh—we've still got some pizza in the fridge." She started to get up. "You want some?"

Molly patted her belly. "I couldn't eat another thing."

Paige relaxed back into the sofa. "Well, it's always there for breakfast then. It'll need using."

Molly noted that Paige was like the traditional Estarian Mom. The Mom she never had.

Paige had a new thought. "Hey, you know what I noticed when Nickie was up here too?"

"What?"

"You're not going to like it…"

Molly narrowed her eyes. "So why tell me?"

Paige twirled at her glass. "Because it amused me," she said simply.

"Go on."

Paige sniggered to herself, her head dropping over her drink and hiding her face. "I just figured that I'd never see anyone that could make you look like you had a stick up your ass!"

Molly burst out laughing, a little bamboozled by the comment. "Well, wonders never cease. I dunno what to tell you."

The laughter settled. "I'm just glad that things are going to be getting back to normal around here."

Just then the airlock popped open at the front door, spilling Arlene and Ben'or out into the foyer. They were laughing and joking, and from what Molly could tell, propping each other up.

"Well, almost normal," she added.

Just then Joel appeared at the kitchen door with the beer, but Molly's attention was pulled by the Estarian-Zyhn couple who had just appeared.

"Just going to take a pod back down to Estaria," Arlene called over from the foyer as the pair staggered through. "That okay?"

Molly waved her hand. "Sure. Be safe, night!"

Arlene and Ben'or, still giggling like teenagers headed for the basement door and helped each other down.

Molly shook her head, smiling. "They make a good couple."

Paige eyed her knowingly. "Yes," she agreed, looking up at Joel who had returned from the kitchen. "A good couple." She shuffled up off the sofa and stood. "I'm gonna go find Maya. She's taking way too long to find that bottle we stashed. I suspect she's just opened it herself!"

She clipped away across the foyer disappearing down the corridor to the quarters.

Joel sat down in the armchair across from Molly. "Soooooo," he drawled nervously. "Nickie makes you look like you have a stick up your ass?"

Molly sniggered, taking another sip of her beer. "You heard that?" She snorted lightly. "I guess so. All the more reason I'm glad she's gone."

Joel grinned. "Well, I think you handled the whole thing pretty well."

"Thanks," she said, raising her bottle to Joel.

"Tell you what," he offered. "Lemme go and drop these beers back downstairs and then I'll come back up to hang for a bit. Things are getting a bit intense down there on the MMORPG game that Oz and Bourne decided to run together."

Molly sniggered again. "I can only imagine!"

"Yeah, I'll tell you about it. Gimme a few minutes." He got up and carried the beer away, leaving her to sit alone in contemplation for a few minutes.

It's not often I'm on my own these days, she noted to Oz.

Oz?

No response.

Oz?

Yeah. I get it. But, erm, can we hang later. I'm in the middle of—

Your role-playing game.

Yes. And Bourne is being a little arse, so I need to show him who's boss.

Molly, tipsy and happy, giggled to herself. *Ok, Oz. May the force be with you.*

She sat for a few moments, appreciating everything she had in her life: her team, her friends, and missions that meant something. Missions that could make a difference.

Doesn't get much better than this, she thought to herself.

What? His tone was intense and distracted.

Nothing, Oz. I'm thinking to myself.

Right. Okay, Bye.

And he was gone again.

EPILOGUE

Ekks Residence, Spire, Estaria

Richard Ekks slowly came aware of the world, the comfort-ableness of his dream floating away as the bleeping sound tore him back to reality. He felt a wave of nausea move through his exhausted body.

Reluctantly he opened his eyes. They stung. He reached across to the bedside table to lift his holo.

Four in the morning.

Fuck.

It was an incoming call. He didn't recognize the address, which meant it was likely *him*.

Hurriedly he sat up and readied himself for the interaction. He wiped his hand over his face and tapped accept.

"Are you able to talk?" The voice on the other end was clipped, but calm. It was Ghetti.

"Yes. I'm alone," Ekks responded.

"We have something else for you to do."

"Okay."

"We need you to make sure that the warships are launched and protecting the outer system."

Richard felt another wave of nausea hit him. This time it wasn't from exhaustion.

"How do you expect me to do that?" He tried to keep his voice steady, but felt it crack as the air seemed to disappear from his lungs.

"We made you Commander of the Estarian-Ogg Space Fleet for a reason. Did we make a mistake?"

Ekks felt his mind whirring. He needed to stay on point. He could process later. "I need support from the Senate. Consensus from my peers. I can't just launch them. There are practicalities to consider."

"This is your task," the voice told him.

"But you don't understand. I can't just—"

"You can." Ghetti was eerily firm. "Do what you need to do to make it happen."

There was a slight pause as Ekks thought through what he had to do. "It's going to take some time," he said quietly.

On the other end of the call Raj Ghetti smiled, satisfied, with cool confidence. The discussion of the parameters was merely an indication that he had already accepted the task. "You have a few months. Start the process. But don't put off acting. When the time comes we are going to need those ships in position. Our very existence in this system will depend on it."

"I understand." Ekks made an effort to sound in control, when in reality he had no idea what was happening or what he was really going to do.

"Good. I'll be in touch."

The call was ended.

Ekks sat in his darkened bedroom, palpitations thumping through his chest and throat, threatening to give him a heart attack.

He thought he could handle the pressure. He thought he had been acting in the greater good when Ghetti had first pitched him the opportunity. But now, faced with the task of launching the ships with no immediate threat, he couldn't help but wonder what he'd signed up for.

What was he going to be forced to do in the coming weeks and months?

FINIS

HOLO TRANSMISSION FROM OZ

Greetings of the day upon you.

Oz here.

Molly has asked me to be the liaison between her operation and your rather primitive earth communication methods.

I believe you call it *email?*

Still.

I am here to act as your interface. To help bridge the gap between the dopamine induced hits as you watch Molly through her trials and tribulations as she takes on all manner of shenanigans.

If you'd like to receive such status updates, please go ahead and leave your holo/ email address here:

http://ellleighclarke.com/

As you might have gathered, this transmission will not just be coming through space between our two galaxies, but is also traveling back through time.

I will attempt to send you updates in chronological order but do be advised that occasionally gravitational optics will interfere (no pun intended!) with the sequencing of these packets.

An understanding of all things timey-whimey will be useful in such instances.

Additionally, if you have any feedback for Molly - or her team - do feel free to pass that on through me. All you need to do is hit reply to any of my messages.

I process every communication personally.

Looking forward to hearing from you.

Oz

(on behalf of Molly, *aka the lady- boss)*

Sanguine Squadron 2.0

Gaitune-67,

Sark System,

Loop Galaxy

AUTHOR NOTES - ELL LEIGH CLARKE
MAY 2ND, 2018

Thank Yous

As always big thanks must go to MA for his continued support, and encouragement. The truth is, I hate writing in isolation, and even though we don't agree on a lot of things (like whether he wrote Nicky or Nickie in the original short story about Nicky Grimes) it still means a lot to have someone there to sound board with and read the stories when I get to the 75% done mark and losing the will to put fingers to keyboard. Somehow that always seems to help.

<Mike Edit: I feel like SUCH a louse! I've had to ask Ellie to push through for the last week mostly alone as I work on Payback Is a Bitch. In fact, they had two issues I needed to look at and both fell asleep before I woke up from my nap. >

Make no mistake, as much as I ADORE telling stories and weaving intricate plots... writing all the words, all the time, is exhausting. Some days I feel like I've run a marathon.

And MA is always there at the other end of slack to... well, laugh at me, and tell me everyone is in the same boat. ;) (I was gonna say hand me water and give me a pep talk. I guess he does that sometimes too.)

<Mike Edit: Here is a glass of the bestest H20 Ever. GO ELLIE, GO!>

Massive thanks must also go to our awesome JIT team and Zen-Steve. I'm immensely grateful to them all for their hard work in turning this around and making it happen in time for our deadline. I also truly appreciate how much our JIT team cares. I mean, here we are, ten books in, and they still want this to be the best, most consistent version of itself that we can possibly put out. It's touching to know how hard you guys work on something that is a passion and not a job. I deeply appreciate you.

So now I have a confession:

I'm just hoping that Steve doesn't have time to notice that one of the baddies has the same name as him. When I checked with MA I was keen that Steve didn't think that I was naming this sneaky psychopath after him – because they are truly nothing alike. It's just I needed a name beginning with S, and Steve is what came to mind.

<Steve Edit: I did notice, and I've lost sleep wondering what it was I'd done to upset you>

I hope we're still cool, Zen-Steve!

<Mike Edit: I totally did tell her that Steve wouldn't mind. He goes by Stephen on Facebook. It's really not the same guy.>

<Steve Edit: I totally don't mind, but wanted to at least inflict some minor sneaky psychopath level emotional pain ;)>

I also owe an immense debt of gratitude to you the reader who reads the stories (sometimes more than once!), writes the five start reviews, and provide an endless source of encouragement over on the facebook page. The 5* reviews also mean that the Amazon algorithms show the book to more readers. I've seen some statistics recently from someone who works at Amazon. Your reviews mean everything in terms of us being picked up by more readers, and you have no idea what it means to me that you take the time to do it. Thank you!

I'd also like to say a huge thank you to everyone on my fb page.

Even when I drop off the radar for a few weeks, you're still there when I come back. That is huge. Your support and friendship means the world to me, and when fun shit happens I wanna get photos. Why? So that I can show you what else is going on behind the scenes of the Sanguine Squadron!

I've said it before, but I'll say it again: You keep me writing.

Without you, these stories would not be told. <3

E x

MA vs Nickie. And Nicky

Sometimes there is reason for MA to get involved in the manuscript for these books. Mostly when it bumps up against Federation stuff. As you probably know, Nicky Grimes comes firmly in the camp of "Federation Stuff", so when MA had a read of it, there were things that needed... tweaking.

So over a day or so MA goes through the various references to Nicky and about 11.30 last night I got a call.

MA: I don't understand why you've made Nicky into such a pussy!

Ellie: I didn't. What do you mean by pussy?

MA: Blah blah blah. Blah blah blah. <Mike Edit: Please insert VERY intelligent arguments here. Cogent, hard to counter-argue...You know, bulllshit!>

Ellie: well, compared to Molly she's very laid back, but I wouldn't say she was a pussy. Change the bits you want to.

The call goes on for about twenty minutes, then we agree he's going to make some more tweaks. We hang up.

Ten seconds later, he's calling again.

Ellie: Did you just pocket dial me?

MA: No. I was just calling to say that I changed five words and we're all ok now. <Mike Edit: It was 7 words...That's like 40% more...>

Ellie: (pisses herself laughing and hangs up.)

Oh! But that's not even the point of this section. There's more.

As you may be aware MA and I have been talking about doing a cross series with Nicky and Tabitha. Kinda a Ranger Two thing that crosses time. Anyway, we both have waaaay too much writing to do already, so it's on the back burner for now, but probably still happening at some point.

Anyway, we've worked on this, and I've thrown together a bunch of beats for my part. But in order for this to work, I needed to do a shit tonne of research on Nicky – which meant reading her short story in Pew Pew.

Which I did.

Despite my inability to read fast.

In it, I made a bunch of notes. Like how to spell Grimm'Zee and which spelling he used for Nicky.

Then, I get a message from him on slack, saying I've spelled Nickie wrong!

I make my case, but when I get the manuscript back, he's changed about half of them back to Nickie.

All I can say is thank goodness for the "find and replace" function.

MA vs Tony Robbins

The other week MA and I were discussing things that needed to be done in the business. I think I'd suggested something, and I asked if he'd remember to do it. (Not that he often forgets, but well.. er.. anyway…)

<Mike Edit: Yes…yes I do and Ellie is very patient with me right now… Probably way more than I deserve.>

He confidently waved a dark covered a4 book in front of the camera. "I've got myself a calendar," he declared with the vigor of someone who might well have just acquired the Ring of Mardoor.

Oh, great! I said, encouragingly.

"It's a Tony Robbins one," he told me. "I'm going to be more motivated and on top of things than Mr. Motivation himself."

I tried to hide my smile. He was about to tell me the story about how he'd been recommended it, but I guess my teasing had already begun.

"Great! so this means you're never going to forget anything ever again?"

He blushed and nodded, quietly writing in it now.

"And this means you're ready to conquer the world?" I asked.

He said something to the affirmative.

I assumed that this would mean that he won't forget important things going forward. That he's all over projects faster than a rash of poison ivy. That he's like a steel trap ready to spring into action at a moment's notice, with all the information at his finger tips.

Well...

The following week I asked him about something we'd agreed to put into play, and he hadn't done it.

"But it was in your Tony Robbins calendar!" I protested.

"Yeah, yeah. You're fully at liberty to say I told you so!"

"I would never be that obvious," I told him, secretly knowing he'd just given me more fodder for the trials and tribulations that I could share in our Author Notes for your amusement.

<Mike Edit: Dammit!>

Seals vs Lobsters

As you know, I'm completely baffled by human kind. I guess that's one reason why I write science fiction – a commentary on how we operate as societies as we tweak the playing field with technology. There are very few things that make sense to me... particularly around how humans can do awful things to each other.

Competition I kinda get – in a more intellectual sense. But not to the extremes that I've seen guys screw themselves over to make a point.

<Mike Edit: Ellie admits right here that she just doesn't get guys. But, that's true of a lot of women…Ellie is just more scientifically curious as to WHY she didn't get guys. So, she reads about lobsters.>

Anyway, recently I've been reading the popular book by one of the greatest intellectuals of the modern era. He's recently become a youtube sensation, but don't let that put you off. He's one of the few folks who can articulate ideas that if we only stopped to think about, we might stand a better chance of interacting more productively. I know he's also controversial, but I think that is a function of trying to have a real and honest conversation in an ecosystem that operates in polarized sound bites.

Quite how he's managing to overcome this, is fascinating.

So I've been reading his book – which he touts as a self-help book. Mostly for young males. But I've found it incredibly instructive already. In talking about the lobster in the context of evolutionary theory of behavior I finally understand much better why people operate the way they do: why guys get cross when they lose at poker, why they'll go to extraordinary lengths to screw each other over in business. Why what people think about them is more important than anything else… including survival, and so on.

Anyway, one day I was talking with MA and happened to mention this. Apparently I went on about the details for a while. What can I say – it was a revelation for me.

<Mike Edit: And by while, I think an hour…>

A few days later he wanted to refer back to some of the points I'd made in this discussion, but he couldn't quite remember the word 'lobster'.

MA: You know, that stuff that's delicious.

Ellie: frowns.

MA: Seals... or something?

Ellie: Seals are delicious?

MA: No... lobsters. I mean lobsters.

Ellie: Hang on, let's go back to the bit where you think seals are delicious....

Another intellectual discussion derailed at it's inception.

<Mike Edit: OMG! That is TOO FUCKING FUNNY. Well, shit. I will have to admit it's true though.>

It's all coming up sea food

At the tail end of a conversation where MA was talking about going to get food or something. In his defense it was probably a bad line and he may have been walking.

Ellie: also, we need to sort out covers for Molly.

MA: ugh I hate that stuff.

Ellie: huh? What stuff?

MA: that sea food.

Ellie: (completely baffled and intrigued by what he thought she'd said): what has seafood got to do with book covers?

MA: wait. What do you say before?

Ellie: I said we needed to sort out covers for Molly.

MA: oh, shit. I thought you'd said calamari.

Ellie: (facepalm) It's ok. It was my fault for trying to talk to you when you were hungry.

<Mike Edit: HAHAHAHAHAHAHA....>

Exploding Kittens

The other week I had a friend from LA staying with me while he was attending a conference nearby. One evening we ended up at one of his other friend's places in another part of town. So there we were, drinking wine, sitting in the living room, when someone (maybe Ellie) notices a box of cards under the tv that said something like Exploding Kittens on it.

I had no idea what they were, so Pelin got them out to show

me and explained to me that it's a game. As we'd had a few drinks already someone suggested we played it.

Now, I'm not normally one for games, but since my attempts to assimilate with people have led me to playing poker and Cards Against Humanity,... and because everyone else wanted to play, I figured, what did I have to lose.

Now my friend from LA is a business strategist, amongst other things. He's kinda hard core and a serious entrepreneur. These personality traits seem to be transposed over to games too because the next thing I realize is that he's pulling up a video about the rules so that he doesn't have to bother remembering them correctly and what ensues is a game more strategic than chess!

And taken waaay more seriously than anyone should take a game with exploding kitties on the cards.

Well, it turned out that actually it is quite strategic and for a kid's game takes quite a bit of cognitive processing.

I was so impressed with it I ended up mentioning it at the next poker game and I managed to generate enough interest to warrant buying a pack and bringing them to the game the following week.

I was a bit nervous, because these guys are hard core poker players. Some of them wear glasses so you can't see their eyes. Some shuffle like they've done this professionally. Many have won tournaments in Vegas with big prize money.

On the surface they can be a little intimidating.

Last week I managed to grab a few players who had been knocked out, and in the hiatus between being knocked out and starting the cash game I suggested we play.

Now whether they were humoring me, or they'd had too much beer to be able to say no...we'll never know.

But we started.

We got as far as watching the video and setting up the cards, but then it was time for the cash game, so they had to go away again.

I'm planning to keep them in my bag for next time, but I think it's already generated enough interest and amusement to get a game going another time.

It also reminded me of the scene from Buffy the Vampire Slayer, where Spike took Buffy to his underground poker game where the demons were playing for kittens!

Alcohol poisoning

Turns out alcohol poisoning is a thing, not just reserved for underage drinkers at prom.

I went out the other night and had four margaritas over the course of five hours. I was home by midnight, and not even slurring my words. And yet, what followed for the following 24 hours was horrendous.

I'll spare you the details, but I survived.

I wondered if my drink had been spiked by something. It's possible, but then, what would have been the point, because I was up all night and didn't pass out. Not even close.

The only other thing that happened was that my friend complained about the drinks not being the same as the first lot, so the bar tender added some tequila. We ended up going back to the same bar tender each time, and then taking our drinks back into where the band was. I wonder if they were just over-'egging' the drinks, maybe.

When I told one of my friends (who is an experienced partier) he said that dehydration can be a big problem. "You're in Austin now, honey!" he reminded me.

So that's it. Either I never drink again, which was my first inclination… Or I just have to be super careful to not over do it, and make sure I drink water.

Basically all the things we're told as teenagers.

Go figure.

Poker vs the Late Night Booty Call

So for the first time ever, I needed to cash out of the cash game in poker this week. (We play a tournament first and then while that finishes those of us who have been knocked out play a cash game.)

Normally I just play until I have no more chips left – in both cash and torney.

But this time was different.

I didn't know the protocol.

So I asked.

Big mistake.

Jason: Why are you cashing out Ellie?

John: Why are you leaving now Ellie?

Nick: Ellie's got a booty call! I saw her on her phone a minute ago!

(*OMG. Could these guys be any more embarrassing?*)

Ellie: No. no I haven't. I'm just going to meet a friend.

(*Nick, Jason, et al... All jeering and teasing.*)

Ryan (the wise one): What I don't understand is why you're not giving them shit back, Ellie. Nick said that like he was surprised. Why would he be surprised that you've hooked up? Eh Nick?

Nick shuts up.

Ellie says her goodbyes and leaves, now knowing:

1. how the lobster mind responds to winning and losing,
2. how to shut a poker player up in short order.
   (Although, I suspect this turning things around on a guy is something that most females have already mastered by the time they're wearing a training bra. I'm sure I'm behind the curve on some of these things, but thank goodness for the good guys who can teach me in a relatively controlled, and safe environment!)

AUTHOR NOTES - MICHAEL ANDERLE
WRITTEN MAY 2, 2018

First, THANK YOU for not only reading our story, but now my little Author Notes after the amazing version Ellie just supplied.

I suck.

Actually, I'm behind on writing a book and writing my Author Notes after Ellie gave me DAYS to finish them was just horrible. I have no idea why I didn't remember to do them Sunday night.

Hell, I hope that I didn't do them and forgot; that shit would be tragic. We are talking past Romeo and Juliet-level stuff here if I write these and then find out I forgot that I had done them already.

You know, Ellie is one of the most decent individuals I know, and certainly the smartest. I do give her a bit of trouble sometimes about what I would perceive is a given, but she will keep focusing on why it just isn't "right."

<<Ellie Edit: you make me sound like I have some innate sense of morality or something. Which isn't quite accurate. But I wont interject a long rant/ discourse on my thoughts on that right here... You're clearly gearing up to make a point. >>

Like Lobsters.

If you haven't read her Author Notes, you really must. Otherwise, what I'm going to write here will make absolutely no sense at all.

No, go ahead, I'll wait…

Ok, you back? Good!

So, Ellie has been pro-humanity con-stupidity (read that as leaning toward why-can't-we-all-just-get-along) ever since I have known her.

<<Ellie: ok, I suppose that is accurate. And an amusing way of putting it. Go on…>>

Not that I knew that originally. What I knew originally was that Sean Platt knew her from an Internet Mastermind group he was involved in.

I learned the above PHCS focus during our effort to work the beats on The Ascension Myth (I just pronounced it correctly in my mind, Ellie…just saying.) and I LIKE to work the feels of my collaborators into our story, or it doesn't resonate.

<< Ellie Edit: hahaha – he normally calls it the AXE-cension myth! >>>

However, I did feel that perhaps Ellie and I would never see eye-to-eye on things about humanity and reality. However, I have always admired her perseverance in her beliefs.

Even when I told her to "Michael Bay the shit out of that scene!" I knew deep down she didn't understand why to do it.

<< Ellie Edit: true. Killy-killy isn't my bag. But I do remember you having that conversation with me having asked a bunch of cops where the best pizza in Austin could be found! >>

Cheese vs. Pepperoni Pizza

One of the best ways to exemplify this is one argument we had about a year ago (can you believe that Ellie has put out ten Molly Books, two Giles books and two Dark Messiah books in twelve months?)

TAKE, THAT GRRM! (George R R Martin—Game of Thrones.)

(Personally, I understand if GRRM is freaking out because of the stress of 'getting it right' with his next book. I wouldn't trade my life for his right now for any amount of money. If that isn't his problem? Well, then I've not a clue why it is taking him so long to produce his next book.)

Ok, back to pizza.

Ellie is all about cheese pizza. Part of it is her no-meat diet focus.

I, of course, am about laying down a good layer of pepperoni on the top, letting the meat melt, the oils from the pepperoni fat soak under the cheese, mixing in with the marinara sauce (no chunks of tomatoes! That's apostasy.)

Finally, the pepperoni will curl up, the edges blackened and crispy so that when I bite into them I hear a crunch when the explosion of flavors hits the back of my mouth.

Not the same as biting into a cheese pizza.

Which is a good metaphor for books without explosions.

I'm a guy, I want explosions...

I do like looking at trouble and how to solve issues from multiple directions. I will admit—without the need for torture—that solving problems intellectually IS the better solution.

But...lobster brain.

The lobster brain in me wants EXPLOSIONS! BIG FANTASTIC EXPLOSIONS WITH body parts and spaceship parts and lots of (enemy) gore flying everywhere!

<< Ellie Edit: yeah this is where I go back to taking intellectual notes. I have no concept of why this is a satisfying thing. >>>

Definitely enemy gore, not good-guys gore.

<< Ellie Edit: and this was a pattern I spotted and replicated from your books. But honestly, do you have ANY idea how unrealistic this is? If something was going down, bombs or guns, or

whatever, the probability that only those on one side, or with a certain set of moral rules, would get hurt is slim. Also – who is to say who are bad and good... Oh yes. The author. But it's still kinda arbitrary in the big scheme of things. I mean, how do the bullets know to just miss the good guys? >>

Until recently, post lobster video, Ellie and I had NO ability to cognitively discuss our pizza issues.

<< Ellie Edit: I think he means pre-lobster reading. It was in a book. But that's a minor point. (Yes, I read something, but to qualify my non-reading thing, I do ok with non-fiction) >>

She was cheese, I was pepperoni.

The two were not going to meet.

Now, after Ellie watching said video and explaining what it meant to her to understand the issue, I am finding it so much easier to discuss our pizza disagreement.

(Our conversation regarding her watching and understanding the video was enlightening in and of itself. I rather wish we HAD captured that first hour as she explained to me what helped her understand the missing link such that both cheese and pepperoni lovers would come out of our 'revelations' video understanding the frame of mind of the other party so much better.)

<< Ellie Edit: hahaha – *first* hour! >>

But, alas, we didn't. We might have been able to bring about World Peace had we put that conversation up on YouTube.

Opportunity lost.

Either way. I am now much more aware that my confusion with Ellie had nothing to do with Ellie not being willing to see reality (meaning, she could see everything but chose not to believe it.) But rather, she was seeking a biological understanding of why guys liked pepperoni pizza and couldn't find a logical reason.

<< Ellie Edit: no – just any understanding. This evolutionary theory was the first explanation that wasn't circular. >>

'Cause it's fucking delicious, and we are wired that way.

As guys, we don't question the love of our pizza, we just love it. (We can be simple that way.)

Wednesday is Poker Night.

Thursday morning comes around every week, and every week I wonder if my Facebook thread is going to have a comment from Ellie about her previous night.

Why? Because she plays poker on Wednesday nights and she could sell a set of stories just on what goes on with her friends until wee early in the mornings.

Personally, I feel sorry for those who play with her. I'm very aware of two (2) things:

1. She is a genius, and poker IS about learning the rules and the percentages and strategies, not winging the shit out of it.
2. I suck at poker, cause I like winging the shit out of something and the numbers hurt my little brain.

But, the guys at the Wednesday night poker are going to feel sorry for her, her British accent, and teach her the rules of the game.

Because, there is no fucking way she will ever be a challenge to them, right? It takes years to build up a working knowledge of poker...

Those poor fuckers.

<< Ellie Edit: hahaha – One of them thinks he's onto me because he's seen my study materials on the counter in my kitchen. He keeps warning them, but he's like the crazy conspiracy person now that no one takes seriously. >>

They won't know what happened until she is right there, knocking them out time and time again (after the first few weeks of them thinking she just 'got lucky.')

Oh, she got lucky all right. She got lucky they didn't realize how fast she learns shit.

Remember, she went from "I haven't read a fiction book since I was twelve" to BESTSELLING Sci-Fi author in one hundred days with multiple releases.

No one does that because they are lucky, and you don't become good at poker because you are lucky either.

Nope, she is going to be wearing that "#1 Poker Player in Austin" hat when she is on television, sunglasses on, playing with the big kahunas in Atlantic City or in Las Vegas sometime and we will all be cheering her on.

Even the lobsters from her Wednesday night Poker nights.

What am I going to do about it?

WHY JAYNE AUSTIN LOVES POKER...

So, Ellie and I are doing a Jayne Austin set of stories. (Nope, not like Jane Austin the author. Think female James Bond in space with a 60s version of free love.)

Something that is going to Rock and Roll the future—Interplanetary Spy for Hire.

<< Ellie Edit: Wait. Wasn't it interstellar? >>>

One of the things we do when collaborating (and it is so much fun) is discuss our characters and go back and forth on beats and stuff. While working on this series, I'm constantly asking, "how did Wednesday go?" and she tells me the latest on poker.

Then, I'm thinking that we need to put this love of poker into Jayne Austin, cause it's funny as hell and she (Ellie) can add that additional reality to the character that helps the character come alive. I'm stoked about the story and hope we do justice to our vision.

If nothing else, the poker scenes will be accurate.

I wonder if her poker friends want to be in a book?

Thank you SO MUCH for reading and to loving Molly and

everyone here. We have two more stories coming at you to finish The Ascension Myth!

All the best,

Michael

BOOKS BY ELL LEIGH CLARKE

The Ascension Myth
* With Michael Anderle *

Awakened (01)
Activated (02)
Called (03)
Sanctioned (04)
Rebirth (05)
Retribution (06)
Cloaked (07)
Bourne (08)
Committed (09)
Subversion (10)
Invasion (11)
Ascension (12)

Confessions of a Space Anthropologist
* With Michael Anderle *

Giles Kurns: Rogue Operator (1)

<u>Giles Kurns: Rogue Instigator (2)</u>

The Second Dark Ages
with Michael Anderle
Darkest Before The Dawn (3)
Dawn Arrives (4)
Deuces Wild
with Michael Anderle
Beyond The Frontiers (1)
Rampage (2)
Labyrinth (3)
Birthright (4)

BOOKS BY MICHAEL ANDERLE

For a complete list of books by Michael Anderle, please visit:

www.lmbpn.com/ma-books/

All LMBPN Audiobooks are Available at Audible.com and iTunes. For a complete list of audiobooks visit:

www.lmbpn.com/audible

CONNECT WITH THE AUTHORS

Receive updates from Oz by registering your holo/ email
address here:
ellleighclarke.com

Facebook:
http://www.facebook.com/ellleighclarke/

Michael Anderle Social

Website:
http://kurtherianbooks.com/

Email List:
http://kurtherianbooks.com/email-list/

Facebook Here:
https://www.facebook.com/TheKurtherianGambitBooks/